THE
TROJAN
COLT

AN ELI PAXTON MYSTERY

THE
TROJAN
COLT

MIKE
RESNICK

WITHDRAWN

SEVENTH
STREET
BOOKS™

59 John Glenn Drive
Amherst, New York 14228–2119

Published 2013 by Seventh Street Books™, an imprint of Prometheus Books

Cover image © 2013 Shutterstock
Cover design by Nicole Sommer-Lecht

Inquiries should be addressed to
Seventh Street Books
59 John Glenn Drive
Amherst, New York 14228–2119
VOICE: 716–691–0133
FAX: 716–691–0137
WWW.PROMETHEUSBOOKS.COM

17 16 15 14 13   5 4 3 2 1

Library of Congress Cataloging-in-Publication Data

Resnick, Michael D.
    The Trojan colt : an Eli Paxton mystery / by Mike Resnick.
        p. cm.
    ISBN 978–1–61614–789–1 (pbk.)
    ISBN 978–1–61614–790–7 (ebook)
    1. Private investigators—Ohio—Cincinnati—Fiction. 2. Horse racing—Fiction. I. Title.

PS3568.E698T76 2013
813'.54—dc23

                                                                                    2013007139

Printed in the United States of America

To Carol, as always,
and to Dan Mayer,
for encouragement and patience.

1.

It was a hot June day. The air-conditioning wasn't working, the phone hadn't rung all day, and the office was starting to feel like the inside of an oven, so I got up, walked out the door, took the elevator down to the ground floor, and stepped outside.

The air-conditioning wasn't working any better on the outside. It must have been ninety degrees, and ninety in downtown Cincinnati, a couple of blocks from the Ohio River, is like a hundred and ten in the desert. In fact, the humidity can make you long for a hundred and ten degrees of what they call a dry heat.

When the Reds are at home most of my favorite eateries are jammed, but the team was busy being rained out in Philadelphia, so downtown was relatively deserted. I considered stopping for a little Skyline chili, which isn't chili at all but is the world's greatest junk food and is unique to Cincinnati, but it was too damned hot to eat—especially chili—so I caught a bus and got off a block from my apartment.

Marlowe was waiting for me. Marlowe's my dog. I don't like him much, and he's not real fond of me, but we're all either of us has, so we put up with each other. He looked as hot as everybody else. He also looked a little tense, or strained, or anxious, so I put his leash on him and we went out for a walk. He relieved himself on Mrs. Garabaldi's petunias, as usual, and she opened her window and cursed at us in Italian, as usual, and Marlowe looked exceptionally proud of himself, as usual, and then we decided only a crazy man and a crazy dog stayed outside in the sunlight on a day like this, so we went back into the apartment.

Marlowe glared at his food until it cringed into submission, but it was too damned hot to eat, and he finally jumped onto my octogenarian couch and began snoring. I sat down on an easy chair, considered turning on the television, but decided there was probably nothing much on that was worth watching, which meant it was a typical day on cable.

I picked up a Playboy—I'd long since admitted that I didn't buy it for the articles—and began thumbing through it, wondering if Miss August was as hot and uncomfortable under the photographer's lights as I was right where I was sitting, and concluded that she couldn't possibly be.

At some point I nodded off. It was dark when I opened my eyes, and after a minute I realized that the reason I'd awakened was because the phone was ringing. It took me a minute to get up and walk over to it, by which time it had stopped ringing.

I figured as long as I was up, I'd get a beer from the beat-up fridge. I wandered into the kitchen, pulled out a can of Bud, popped it open, and was about to take my first swallow of that beautiful cold fluid when the phone rang again.

I got to it on the third ring.

"Goddamnit, Eli, where the hell have you been?" said a familiar voice.

"Right here."

"I just rang a few minutes ago," said the voice. "There was no answer."

"I was sleeping. It took me awhile to walk over to it."

"Why don't you join the twenty-first century and buy a goddamned cell phone?"

"We owe a gazillion dollars and two-thirds of the world wants to kill us, and you enjoy this century?" I said. "I could have picked a better one out of a hat."

"Yeah, if there was ever any doubt about it, now I know I'm talking to the real Eli Paxton."

"And who the hell am I talking to?" I growled.

"Bill Striker, goddammit!"

That woke me up in a hurry. Bill Striker ran the biggest detective agency in Cincinnati. He had a staff of fifteen, plus a pair of secretaries and a receptionist. Of all the detectives in town, he made the most money, had the classiest clients, wore the best suits, drove the most expensive cars, and had the prettiest wife and most accomplished kids. More to the point, every now and then he sent a job my way, and, as usual, I was in no position to turn down any acts of largesse, and given the pile of overdue bills on my desk, the largesser the better.

"Hi, Bill," I said. "Sorry if I seemed groggy for a minute. I was up all night on a stakeout."

"Is it done?"

"Is what done?"

"The stakeout!" he said in exasperated tones. "Have you been drinking?"

"Not today and not enough," I said. "I'm just sleep-deprived." And cash- deprived, I added silently. "Anyway, the stakeout's over."

"Good," said Striker. "I'm in a position to throw you a little work. Pays pretty well for what it is."

"Okay, what is it?"

"Security," he replied.

"Rock star or athlete?"

"A horse."

"Okay, it's my turn to ask you," I said. "Have you been drinking— or has this horse maybe swallowed some diamonds?"

"He's worth more than diamonds—potentially, anyway," said Striker. "I know you live and die with the Reds and the Bengals . . ."

"Hell, everyone dies with the Bengals," I said.

"But I also know you go out to the track every now and then."

"Yeah, I do," I said. "But there's nothing running at River Downs that's worth a bodyguard, and besides, your agency's got a starting lineup that could spot the Bengals two touchdowns and still beat them."

"And most of them are going to be doing exactly what you're doing, Eli," said Striker.

"Okay, I'm wide awake and still mystified," I said. "Explain, please."

"You're right about River Downs," he said. "But we're not talking about River Downs."

"What are we talking about?"

"Try ninety miles south of here," said Striker. "The Keeneland Summer Sale starts next week. The Striker Agency has been hired to provide security for some of the well-bred yearlings, a few of which will sell for well over a million dollars."

I'd heard of the sales, of course, even read about them, but ninety miles was as close as someone of my social and financial stature ever got to them. These were the high rollers of the thoroughbred industry, guys who would risk a couple of million to buy a well-bred or good-looking yearling that had never raced, maybe even never been saddled.

"Don't they have round-the-clock grooms for these babies?" I asked, hoping he'd say no. "I mean, I figure the groom probably sleeps in the stall with the horse."

"They know how to care for horses," replied Striker. "They don't know shit about providing security."

"Have there been any threats?"

"No one's going to kill one of these yearlings, Eli," said Striker, as if speaking to a child. "What they may do, if they can get away with it, is steal one. Then they have two options: put a look-alike ringer in the stall, keep the yearling themselves, and hope he runs true to his pedigree. But in truth that's awfully far-fetched. What's far more likely is that they'll just disable or bribe the groom, take the horse away, and hold him for ransom."

"I suppose that figures. What breeder wouldn't pay a quick couple of hundred grand and agree to drop all charges to get his million-dollar yearling back?"

"You got it," said Striker. "So, you want to bodyguard a colt and his groom for a week? Double your usual fee, room and board comped, reimbursement for gas."

"Yeah, I'm in. Any idea who I'm guarding?"

"Remember Trojan?"

"Remember him?" I shot back. "Hell, I damned near went broke trying to find a horse to beat him."

"He was really something," agreed Striker. "Unbeaten at two, won the Derby at three, Horse of the Year at four, retired with earnings of almost eight million dollars. He was syndicated for about forty-five million." There was a pause. "Damn! I still remember that Preakness. Stumbled at the start, blocked at the head of the stretch, he didn't get loose until the last hundred yards, and he still came within length of winning it. I hate to tell you how much I lost on that race."

"He was some horse," I agreed. "But surely he's not up for sale."

"No, this is a yearling sale," said Striker. "Besides, Trojan has been syndicated, split into forty-five shares. They can't sell him, just parts of him."

"So who *am* I guarding?"

"The first Trojan colt ever to make it to the auction ring," answered Striker. "I think there'll be two more sold at Saratoga in a couple of months, and there are three fillies up for sale at Keeneland, but most people are hanging on to their Trojans."

"That sounds one step away from being a dirty joke," I said. "When I was a young man, Trojans were—"

"I think they still are," said Striker. "Try to leave your bad taste in Cincinnati."

"When do I leave?"

"Day after tomorrow. I don't suppose you have an e-mail address?"

"Not if you need a computer to have one," I said.

"Figures," he said. "All right, I'll have a messenger drop off the pertinent details at your office tomorrow: where you go, where you stay, who you report to, the usual."

"I'll be looking for it," I said. "And thanks, Bill."

"Happy to do it, Eli. Our personalities may not exactly mesh, but you're a damned good detective. That thing you uncovered when you were looking for the show dog, that was just grade-A work."

"And now I'm bodyguarding a horse," I said sardonically.

"I think you may have found your métier," said Striker with a chuckle and hung up.

Marlowe gave me a look that said: So you think guarding a horse is a no-brainer? You just don't know us animals, pal.

In retrospect I should have listened to him.

2.

The first order of business was to find a place to stash Marlowe for a week. Mrs. Garabaldi was out of the question. I could almost see her horrified expression: "*Me?* You want *me* to take care of the petunia killer?"

The only other little old lady I knew was Mrs. Dorfmeyer, but she had a pair of cats that Marlowe would have eaten for breakfast. Finally I phoned the huge kennel just north and east of town, but when I found out what it would cost to board him for a week, I decided I could either find a neighbor who was willing to watch him for a few days (which meant a neighbor who didn't know him), or I'd take him with me and let him spend a week growling and terrifying all the million-dollar yearlings.

I took him for a walk when I got home, and Fate intervened, because I ran into Mrs. Hoskins just as Mrs. Garabaldi was cursing both Marlowe and me for what he'd done yet again to her petunias.

"Terrible woman!" muttered Mrs. Hoskins.

"It's a comfort to know I'm not the only one who thinks so," I replied.

"She's the cheapest woman in town. My Nancy is helping pay her tuition by waiting on tables. Do you know what Mrs. Garabaldi tipped her for a nine-dollar sandwich and a cup of coffee? A quarter!"

"I'm almost sorry Marlowe won't be able to soil her flowers for a week."

She looked at me curiously.

"I'm leaving town on business. I'll have to board him."

"Board him?" she repeated.

"I can't take him with me."

"I'll tell you what, Mr. Paxton," she said. "If you leave him with me for the week, I promise to let him lift his leg on Mrs. Garabaldi's flowers at least three or four times a day."

"You mean it?" I asked with a big grin.

She nodded her head vigorously, and her grin matched my own.

"You might as well take him right now," I said, handing her the leash.

"Doesn't he have his own food and water bowls?"

"He'll eat and drink out of anything."

"And toys?"

"Give him an old shoe," I said. In fact, try to keep one away from him. It can't be done.

She took the leash, began talking baby talk to Marlowe—who pretended he didn't mind—then asked me if I'd like to kiss him good-bye. I explained that it just wasn't manly, and she accepted it, which is probably why I still have a nose, as Marlowe tends to bite anything smaller than himself.

I walked back to the apartment, began packing, finally turned on the TV, cracked open a beer, and fell asleep sometime during the third inning. When I woke up the game was over, and the channel was running an old Bette Davis film, so I tried to get the score from some other channel, but the only thing I learned from MSNBC was why only right-wing idiots work for Fox News, and the only thing I learned from Fox News was why only left-wing whackos work for MSNBC. I tried ESPN, but they were showing reruns of a Little League game in New Mexico, and finally I fell asleep again.

The next morning I got into the Ford, which was even older in car years than I was in people years, and began driving south on the Interstate. I drove past the Great American Ballpark (which everyone still calls Riverfront Stadium) and Paul Brown Stadium, across the Ohio River into Kentucky, and past the Cincinnati Airport (which is legally part of Cincinnati, for reasons known only to select Kentucky politicians and their bankers). I stayed on I-75 after it branched off from I-71, all the way down to Lexington, where the grass really isn't blue but the horses' blood sure as hell is.

I'd been told to report to Ben Miller, one of Striker's higher-ups, at the Hyatt on West High Street. I pulled up, turned the car over to a valet, and decided this might not be such a mundane job after all. Stand guard over a yearling during the day, dine in the four-star restaurant here, then take an elevator up to my room, shower away all the smell of horses and stables, and go to sleep without Marlowe snoring on the other pillow.

I was ten feet inside the door when Miller walked up to me, hand extended.

"Good to see you, Eli," he said. "It's been awhile."

"Hi, Ben." I looked around the lobby. "Nice headquarters. I approve."

He chuckled at that and shook his head. "This isn't our headquarters, Eli. I just chose it because it's so easy to find." He paused long enough to make sure I wasn't going to break down and cry. "No, we'll be staying at Keeneland."

"The racetrack?" I said, surprised.

"Well, the barns, anyway."

"The whole time?"

"Until the auction starts. Then each of us will accompany our horse to the sales pavilion. Once it's sold, we're no longer responsible for it."

"Where do we eat and sleep?" I asked.

He smiled. "You'll see."

"I hope you're not about to tell me that I have to sleep in the stall with a horse," I said.

Another chuckle. "Not even the grooms do that. Well, hardly any of them, anyway." He glanced out the window, where a Lincoln limo had just pulled up. "Ah! Here are four of the guys from the agency. Excuse me a moment while I greet them."

Then he was out the door, and I took another look around the luxurious lobby. Good-bye, Hyatt, I thought. We could have had something special—but I'm leaving you for a horse.

I'm sure if the hotel could have answered, it would have sighed deeply and said, You aren't the first.

Miller left his little group and walked over to me.

"Looks like we may have a transportation problem, Eli," he said. "Too many of us, too few cars. Think you can follow us to Keeneland?"

I shrugged. "How hard can it be?"

He handed me two small pieces of cardboard. "Stick this inside your car window," he said. "It'll get you free parking."

"And this one?" I asked, holding up the other ticket.

"It'll get your meals comped at the track kitchen."

"You weren't kidding," I said. "I'm really supposed to sleep in the stall."

He shook his head. "In the barn. They've set up a tack room for you."

"And all the other security sleeps in the Hyatt?"

He sighed. "Not a chance. You know how many goddamned barns there are at Keeneland?"

"Okay," I said. "But if these horses are worth half what everyone seems to think they're worth, they should be sleeping at the Hyatt."

"We'll bring it up to Fasig-Tipton next year."

"Fasig-Tipton?"

"That's the company that runs the sale," answered Miller. "I've already sent for your car," he continued, as the Ford sputtered up to the door. "Just follow the limo to the track, and then ask someone to show you the way to Barn 9."

He turned and rejoined Striker's employees. I followed them out, tipped the valet, got in the Ford, stuck in a cassette—it wasn't new enough to have a CD player—and listened to Carmen Miranda and the Andrews Sisters sing duets (four-ettes?) all the way to the track.

Keeneland wasn't as overwhelming as Belmont or Santa Anita, and in terms of size it even took a backseat to Churchill Downs an hour's drive to the west, but it was a lovely, parklike setting and it had a storied history, having played host to some of the great horses of the past century. I parked the car—I looked around, but neither of Striker's limos was anywhere near me—and began walking toward the barns. As I approached them a uniformed guard walked up to me.

"May I help you?" he said in a tone that implied he'd be equally happy arresting me.

"My name's Eli Paxton," I said. "I'm supposed to report to Barn 9."

He pulled a little notebook out of his breast pocket. "Paxton ... Paxton," he murmured as he thumbed through the pages. "Ah! Here you are. You're working for the Striker Agency."

I resisted the urge to say "Temporarily," and just nodded my head.

"Follow me, please, Mr. Paxton," he said, turning and leading me to Barn 9.

It took us a couple of minutes to get there, and then we began walking down the aisle between the stalls.

"So where's the other security?" I asked as half a dozen horses stuck their heads over the half doors and stared at us.

"Most of the owners are content to let Keeneland supply it," answered the guard. "I think only eleven yearlings have their own guards."

"The eleven most valuable?" I suggested.

He shrugged. "Today they are. After the auction, who knows?" He came to a stop and looked to his left. "Ah! Here we are."

I looked into the stall. There was a powerfully built chestnut colt—I assumed he was a colt—nibbling on some oats, and in a corner a young guy, either in his late teens or early twenties, was engrossed in reading a magazine.

"Hey, Tony!" said the guard. "Come say hello to Mr. Paxton."

The boy—I could see now that he probably wasn't even twenty yet—stood up and walked over.

"Hi," I said. "I'm Eli Paxton. I'll be keeping an eye on your charge here."

He frowned, puzzled. "My charge?"

"Your horse."

"Oh." Suddenly he smiled and extended a hand, which I took. "I'm pleased to meet you. I'm Tony Sanders."

"Okay, you don't need me any longer," said the guard. "I've got to get back to my post."

"Thanks for your help," I said as he left.

"Well, Mr. Paxton . . ." Tony began.

"Call me Eli," I said.

"Well, Eli, what do you think of him?"

"Very pretty."

He shook his head. "Not pretty. That's for fillies. He's powerful."

"That, too," I agreed.

The colt looked up from his oats, walked over, and nuzzled Tony.

"Damn! I'm going to miss him after he's sold."

"I take it you don't go with him?"

He shook his head. "I work for Mr. Bigelow. He's the breeder. When Tyrone's gone, I'll be given some other horse to rub down."

"Tyrone?" I repeated. "That's an unusual name for a horse."

"Oh, it's just his call name—the name we call him around here. He hasn't got an official name yet. That'll be up to the new owner."

"It's an unusual name anyway."

"It's for Tyrone Power," said Tony. "I guess he was an old-time actor, but I've never seen any of his movies." He made a face. "They say they're mostly in black-and-white."

"So let me use my keen deductive mind and suggest that Mrs. Bigelow loves Tyrone Power movies."

He shrugged. "I don't know. She's got nothing to do with the horses. Mr. Bigelow named him because he says Tyrone Power was always getting into swordfights in the movies."

I looked at the colt. "Which hoof does he hold his sword in?"

Tony laughed. "Here, let me turn him around for you."

He grabbed the colt's halter and gently led him in a semicircle.

"See?" he asked.

The colt had a scar maybe ten or eleven inches long on the right side of his neck.

"What the hell happened to him?" I said.

"We tell everyone that he got into a swordfight, and we had to bury the loser," said Tony with a grin. "But the truth is that a bunch of weanlings were running along one of the fences last winter and he got knocked into one. They still don't know if it was a nail or just a spike of wood, but they say he was bleeding like all get-out, and it took some-thing like forty stitches to close the damned thing." He shrugged. "Still, he's no worse for it. They say either he or that gray colt by Storm Cloud will bring the top price."

"Tyrone," I repeated. "Well, I suppose it could be worse. Could be Jasper."

"A lot of yearlings have names that would surprise you," replied Tony. "They say that Seattle Slew was so big and awkward that they called him Baby Huey after that cartoon bird."

"Well, if a Baby Huey can win the Triple Crown, there's no telling what a Tyrone can do." I paused. "Just out of curiosity, where does one eat around here?"

"The track kitchen," said Tony. "I'll point it out when it's dinnertime."

"Point it out?" I repeated. "Why not just walk over there with me."

He shook his head. "Now that you're here, one of us should always stay with Tyrone."

"I know he's worth a bundle," I said, "but there are cops on the ground, and I know for a fact that there'll be ten other detectives here. Surely you can walk a couple of hundred yards away for a bite."

He looked hesitant.

"Think about it, Tony," I said. "This is the most un-stealable horse on the grounds."

He frowned and stared at me. "What are you talking about, Eli?"

"Why would someone steal a million-dollar yearling?" I said.

He shrugged. "To get him for free, I guess."

"Okay," I said. "And do what with him?"

"Race him."

"Right," I said. "I mean, you wouldn't risk going to jail stealing him so your daughter can ride him around the park."

I pointed to the scar on Tyrone's neck. "Until they learn to do plastic surgery on a racehorse, no one's going to steal a horse that's so easy to identify."

His face lightened up, and he smiled. "I never thought of that."

"So we'll have dinner together?" I said. "My treat." Well, Bill Striker's treat, anyway.

"Sure."

An hour later we walked over to the kitchen and grabbed some hamburgers, then went back to Barn 9 and spent a couple of hours just talking. He liked the same sports teams I liked, lusted for the same top-heavy movie stars, hated the same politicians. He even promised to give Casablanca and The Maltese Falcon a try the next time they were on, and I promised to listen to his favorite rock band (once I remembered its name).

By the time I made my way to the tack room and lay down on the cot they'd supplied for me, I almost felt like I'd found the kid brother I never had.

3.

It's a damned good thing that Tony didn't need much sleep, because for the next two days he must have led Tyrone out of his stall twenty times for the benefit of the zillionaires who were considering bidding for him. There were Wall Street businessmen, a couple of Hollywood actors, and enough Arab sheiks to make you think the jihadists had landed.

Probably they knew what they were looking for, and besides, any one of them could have used a couple of million dollars' worth of tax write-off.

But after they were done, a number of them sent the guys (and two ladies) who did know exactly what they were looking for: nine trainers by my count, five of them already in the Hall of Fame. (That's something I learned from Tony. A horse had to be retired before he's eligible for the Hall, but trainers and jockeys can be voted in while they're still working at their trades.)

Bill Halwell, one of the trainers, wearing his Del Mar tan, or maybe it was his Santa Anita tan, went over Tyrone with his hands, inch by inch.

"So what do you think of him?" I asked.

"Nice horse."

"I have no rooting interest," I said. "I'm just the bodyguard."

He nodded. "Reminds me of his father. Not too long in body, which is good. My experience is that long-bodied horses are often short on stamina. Nice shoulder, straight legs, doesn't toe out." He stared at Tyrone, then nodded again. "Yeah, very nice colt."

"How much do you think he'll bring?"

He shrugged. "That's another union."

"How high will you tell your boss to go?"

"Actually, I've got three bosses interested in this colt," answered

Halwell. "The old days, when a trainer worked for just one owner or stable, are long gone. And as for your question, I'm afraid that's privileged information."

"I'm not going to try to outbid them," I assured him with a smile.

"I know," he said returning the smile. "But if I say twenty million, to name a totally preposterous price for the sake of argument, what's to stop you or the groom here from telling Travis Bigelow to bid nineteen and a half million?"

"Who's Travis Bigelow?" I asked.

He laughed. "I guess you really are just the bodyguard. Bigelow is the man who's put this colt up for auction."

"Well, if one of your owners winds up with him, and he's as good as he's supposed to be," I said, "I hope you'll run him here in the Blue Grass Stakes before the Derby so I get a chance to see him and tell everyone I knew him when."

"First let's find out if he can run up to his looks and his pedigree," said Halwell.

He lingered a few more minutes, then wandered off. I don't think Tyrone was in his stall ninety seconds before Biff Wainwright, who had trained Trojan himself, came by to take a look.

"Looks a lot like his daddy," he said. "But what the hell happened to his neck? He'd better give up long blades for safety razors."

Tony explained what had happened.

"And he doesn't shy away when a horse comes up on that side of him?" persisted Wainwright.

Tony shrugged. "I don't know. I've never seen him on a track. He doesn't shy away from people."

"People didn't give him that scar." Wainwright stared at Tyrone for another moment. "Oh, well, I suppose whoever winds up with him will find out soon enough."

He began walking away. I walked to the end of the shed row to see if anyone else was coming, gave Tony an all-clear sign, and he led Tyrone into his stall, took off the lead shank, and came back out, closing the door behind him.

"I guess it's going to be like this from now until they sell him tomorrow afternoon," I said.

"I suppose so."

"Is this your first sale?" I asked.

He shook his head. "No, but it's my first million-dollar horse. I've only had him for a month, but still, I'll hate to go back to cheap horses with nothing special to their names."

"No reason why you should, if you do a good job with Tyrone," I said. "And you seem to be."

He shook his head sadly "Ain't much of value left at the farm," he said. "Mr. Bigelow's been dispersing his stock over the past couple of years."

"Tired of racing?"

"Not into racing at all. He's always been a market breeder." He shrugged. "Maybe he's just tired of Kentucky. He's getting up in years, and he has to drive half a mile just to get to his mailbox. Maybe he wants to take the missus and live in some high-rise in New York City."

"I don't know," I said, leaning against a wooden wall and watching Tyrone nibble his oats. "If I had a horse that might be worth a couple of million, what would I do—sell him or race him?"

"If you were a sportsman—that's how all these rich folk describe themselves—you'd probably race him. And go broke."

"You don't think he'll be any good on the track?" I asked.

"Who knows?" he said. "I think he'll do fine, but the odds say he won't."

"What odds are they?" I asked. "He's never even set foot on a track."

Tony smiled. "You know how many yearlings have sold for over a million dollars?"

I shook my head. "No."

"More than a thousand. You know how many earned back their purchase price on the track?"

I stared at him. "How many?"

"Six. Know how many became year-end champions?"

"Nope."

"Just one: A. P. Indy, a son of Seattle Slew."

"You really know your stuff, kid," I said admiringly.

"I grew up here. You probably know everything there is to know about the Reds and the Bengals. Me, I was always gonna be too small to play basketball for Kentucky or Louisville, so horse-racing became my sport." He flashed me a guilty smile. "You wouldn't believe how long and hard I cried when I realized that I was going to be too big to be a jockey."

"Poor kid," I said. "Too small to guard LeBron James, too big to ride against Garrett Gomez."

He nodded. "I'm a groom now, but ten years from now I'll be training them." He rubbed Tyrone's muzzle. "Who knows? Maybe someday I'll train one of his kids."

"If he's one of the six in a thousand," I said.

"Oh, he doesn't have to win his purchase price to be worth ten times as much. There's far more money in breeding than in racing."

"Explain, please," I said. "I thought the whole point was winning those six- and seven-figure purses."

"Well, it's great if you can, of course," replied Tony, "but you don't have to win a million dollars to be worth more than that at stud. Let's say that Tyrone never makes it to the Triple Crown races. He runs thirty times, and wins seven, and five of them are stakes races—not the Breeders' Cup or anything like that, but good, competitive races at major tracks. Okay, they retire him after his four-year-old season, and because he's a multiple stakes winner and he's by Trojan and maybe some other Trojan colts and fillies are doing well at the track, they stand him for a twenty-five-thousand-dollar fee."

"That much?" I asked.

"Okay, fifteen thousand, which is dirt cheap for a horse with his breeding and record. He covers a hundred mares a year for three years, before anyone knows if his offspring are any good." Suddenly he grinned. "You see? He's already made a million and a half at stud and he's only seven years old. If he sires a champion or a couple of major-stakes winners, by the time he's ten his fee will be up around $50,000. Now, we're not talking a great sire here, a Seattle Slew or Danzig or Storm Bird, just a good, well-bred one with some stakes-winning offspring. Now do you see how the big money's in breeding and not racing?"

"I do indeed," I said. "How much does a truly top sire stand for?"

"Storm Bird stood for eight hundred thousand and got well over a hundred mares a year. Danzig and A. P. Indy were cheaper; they only got three hundred thousand a pop."

I let out a low whistle. "Okay, I'm properly impressed."

"It's not the part of the game I'm attracted to," added Tony, "but it pays for the part I love."

"Hell, it sounds like it could pay the national debt and have something left over," I said.

"It's more than I'll ever have," said Tony. He paused for a moment. "Is anyone else heading this way?"

I looked out into the aisle. "No."

"Good!" he said. "Maybe I can finally catch up on my reading."

"You're in school?" I said, surprised, since I knew caring for the colt was a full-time job.

He shook his head. "No, I quit the day I turned sixteen. I knew what I wanted to be." He walked out of the stall, entered one of the tack rooms, and emerged with a trio of magazines in his hand. "Thoroughbred Weekly, American Racehorse, and Turf. Gotta keep up."

"Well," I said, "since no one seems to be paying us a visit for the next few minutes, and you're doing your homework, I think I'll pop over to the track kitchen and grab a bite."

"See you later," said Tony. He reentered the stall, sat in a corner with his back propped up against the wooden wall, and began reading. I decided that if they were still publishing Black Mask or Dime Detective, maybe I'd look forward as eagerly to my homework as he did to his.

Ben Miller was seated alone at a table and gestured for me to join him.

"How's it going, Eli?" he asked as I pulled up a chair.

"Easiest money I ever made," I told him.

"Yeah," he said. "Our business is always easy—until it isn't."

I nodded in agreement. "Well, at least I got to meet a few billionaires and a handful of trainers I've admired from a distance."

"Any of 'em dead-set on buying the colt?"

I shrugged. "Who knows? The owners could pay for him with

pocket change, and what trainer wouldn't like to have a colt from Trojan's first crop in his barn?"

"True," he agreed. "Doesn't cost Biff Wainwright a penny if the damned horse never wins a race."

"So am I free to go back to Cincinnati after the colt sells tomorrow?"

"Stick around until the next morning. Maybe the new owner will want to keep you on until the sale ends in four days."

"I'm not spending one more night in the tack room than I have to," I said adamantly.

"Let me see if I can get Bill to pop for a room at the Hyatt," he said. "If not, at least I'll try to put you together with the high bidder and see if he wants you to stay with the colt."

"Fair enough." I ordered a sandwich and a beer. "I wonder what Tyrone will finally go for?"

"Tyrone?" said Miller with a smile.

"For Tyrone Power," I answered. "Because of the scar."

"I'm surprised he's not Errol," said Miller. "Still, if they wanted to do it right, he'd be Basil. From what I've read, Rathbone was the only one of them who actually knew how to fence."

"I gather once they put him out with a trainer, he'll get a new nickname."

"Figures," he said, nodding his agreement. "I doubt he knows to answer to 'Tyrone.' They're beautiful animals, and I love to watch them run, but they aren't the brightest critters God made."

My sandwich arrived—a club that was ninety percent lettuce, and some very small, very shy pieces of turkey hiding under a slice of tomato. I stared at it for a moment, then picked it up and took a bite.

"If a jockey has a weight problem," I said, "he could work it off eating these damned sandwiches."

He chuckled at that. "Well, Eli, I've got to make my rounds and check on all our men. Enjoy your"—he glanced at the sandwich—"whatever it is, and don't feed it to the colt. We want him to live long enough for us to get paid."

He got up, left a tip on the table that was large enough to cover both our meals, and walked out. I left half the sandwich on the plate and followed him a minute later.

I wandered back to Barn 9 and walked down the shed row to Tyrone's stall. Tony nodded to me but didn't say a word. He was frowning and pacing back and forth.

"Are you okay?" I asked. "You look like you just ate a sandwich I walked out on."

No smile, and no answer. His tension was making Tyrone nervous, but he didn't notice until I pointed it out to him. Then he left the stall, securing the door behind him, and he stared at me for a long minute.

"You're really a cop?" he said at last.

"I used to be," I answered. "Back when I lived in Chicago maybe ten or twelve years ago. These days I'm a detective."

He seemed about to say something, then thought better of it, and sat down on a chair, staring off into space.

"I don't know what's bothering you," I said, "but if it'll help to talk about it . . ."

"I gotta think about it," he said.

"Okay, but I just want you to know I'm here for you if there's a problem."

"Thanks, Eli," he said. "I appreciate it. You're going to be around tomorrow, right?"

"Right," I replied.

"There's something I got to talk to you about then."

"How about now?" I suggested.

He shook his head. "There's someone I have to talk to first."

"Okay," I said. "I'll be here whenever you have to talk."

It was obvious that he wanted to be alone, so I went into the tack room and read one of the paperback thrillers I'd brought with me until I fell asleep.

In the morning Tony was gone.

4.

I waited an hour or so, then found one of the other men from Striker's agency and told him he'd better report Tony's disappearance to Ben Miller and have them get another groom over to Tyrone's stall, because I had no idea what he ate or when, and I sure as hell wasn't leading him into the sales ring in five more hours.

Then I sat back and waited. Tyrone seemed calm, and if he missed his oats or any of the special things they fed him, you'd never know it to look at him. He grazed on the straw in his stall, and since there was a bit of normal commotion around the barn—yearlings being led out of their stalls to be examined by owners, trainers, and vets, plus a few older horses who were being taken to the track for their morning workouts, he stuck his head out over the half door and watched them with what I assume was interest.

Miller showed up half an hour later with a redheaded, freckled young man of about twenty.

"Eli, this is Jamie Driscoll. Jamie, say hello to Eli Paxton, who will be keeping the bad guys at bay until the Trojan colt goes to someone else's barn."

Jamie extended a callused hand and took mine in a firm grip.

"Pleasetameetcha," he said, scrunching the greeting into a single word. He nodded his head toward the colt. "Got a name?"

"Tyrone," I said.

He smiled. "I approve."

"You like old movies?" I asked.

"You mean black-and-white stuff?" he said contemptuously. "Never watch 'em."

"My mistake," I said. "When you said you liked the name . . ."

"Tyrone Judson," he replied. "He's a six-foot-ten-inch freshman on the Wildcats."

I stepped away from the stall door.

"Well, you two will want to get acquainted," I said.

He shrugged. "We're going to get unacquainted by dinnertime. He's the headliner in this afternoon's auction." He entered the stall, petted Tyrone for a minute, picked up a brush and rag and began grooming him.

"So what the hell happened, Eli?" said Miller.

I shrugged. "Beats me. The kid was here when I went to sleep and gone when I woke up."

"Did he say anything?"

"Something was bothering him, but he didn't walk to talk about it."

"Girl trouble, probably," said Miller. "That's what it usually is at that age."

"Maybe."

"But you don't think so?"

"I don't know. But we talked a lot the past couple of days, and he never once mentioned girls. His passion was racing."

"Maybe he was upset because in all likelihood he'd be losing Tyrone today."

"Come on, Ben," I said. "Until they get Tyrone in a race, for all you know, you can beat him." I started reeling off Tony's figures about expensive yearlings who earned out their purchase prices, and he held up a hand.

"Okay, okay," he said. "My interest in horses starts and ends at the finish line. Kid probably went out to the West Coast for drugs and sex, just like all the other kids these days. He's not our responsibility."

I could tell Ben wasn't interested in talking about Tony anymore, and Jamie was busy working on Trojan, so I decided I might as well go over to the track kitchen for what I hoped would be my last meal at Keeneland.

A couple of Striker's men were there, but all they wanted to talk about was some owner's sexy wife, who could probably have bought the three of us with the mad money she spent on clothes in a week. Then, since the NFL football training season had begun, the subject changed to arms. It was always arms in the summer in Cincinnati—Ken Anderson's, Boomer Esiason's, Carson Palmer's, and these days Andy Dalton's. Once they started full-contact scrimmages it would turn to knees.

Finally they left. I sat alone with my cup of coffee and what was left of my cheese Danish, and wondered where the hell Tony had gone off to—and, more importantly, why. He had to know that this would be a black mark against him, that no one hires a groom who walks off in the middle of the night, and since he was too big to be a jockey and too poor to be an owner and not anywhere skilled enough to be a trainer, how the hell was he going to find work in this sport that he so clearly loved?

I thought about it until my coffee turned cold and then walked back to the barn. Jamie had finished rubbing Trojan down and was feeding him a carrot when I arrived.

"Welcome back," he said. "Hope you ate well."

"As well as can be expected at a backstretch kitchen," I replied. "I'll be here 'til the auction if you want to go grab some breakfast."

He smiled. "You're new to the track, ain'tcha?"

"To all of it except the two-dollar windows," I said.

"I know. Around here, the day starts at sun-up. Most of the trainers, grooms, and jocks you see had breakfast three hours ago and are starting to think about lunch."

"Thank God I won't be here long enough to get used to those hours," I said devoutly, and he laughed.

"Well, you don't see any of the owners around in the mornings, either," said Jamie.

Somehow it seemed a little early to read the thriller I'd taken to bed the night before, so I picked up some of the racing magazines Tony had been reading and started thumbing through them. I didn't see any ads for the top sires, the champions I remembered from the racetrack, but that figured: they were booked years ahead, so why spend the money on ads? Actually, more than half of the ads were for yearlings that were being sold in the next few days, which certainly made sense. I wondered how many of them would ever be heard of again after the first of the year, the arbitrary birthday of all racehorses. And then I wondered if Tony Sanders would ever be heard of again either. Hell, kids walked off jobs all the time, but there was just something about his face the night before that bothered me. He didn't look bored, or lustful, or high. He looked scared, or at least worried.

I spent a couple of hours trying not to think about him. Thoroughbred Weekly had a fascinating article listing the all-time biggest busts— starting with that thirteen-million-dollar half brother to Seattle Slew who never won a race, and juxtaposing them to the list of the greatest bargains. Twenty-five thousand for John Henry looked pretty good, given that he won over six million, but of course he was a gelding and his earnings stopped the day he left the track. The trick was to buy something like Storm Bird and collect eighty million a year in stud fees.

Anyway, I didn't even notice the time passing by until one of the sales officials stopped at the stall and told Jamie to get Tyrone ready, that he'd be sending an escort over in a couple of minutes, and then they'd all walk to the sales pavilion together.

"Personally," he added, "I think it makes more sense to put the cream of the crop up at night, where fans can watch the auction on streaming video, but two of the people who want to bid on this colt asked for an afternoon auction, since they won't be here tonight. They could use proxies to do their bidding, of course—I mean, hell, we've been doing that for the better part of a century—but I guess they're business rivals and each wants to gloat over the other if he wins the auction."

Then he was gone, and Jamie ran a brush over Tyrone one last time and attached a lead shank to the halter.

"I've gone over every inch of him," he told me, "and there ain't so much as a pimple. I say he brings close to two mil."

"I've heard higher guesses than that," I said.

"That's because he's the first Trojan colt ever to enter the ring," answered Jamie. "But he had a mama too, and every time she ran more than nine furlongs she tripped on her pedigree." He shrugged. "What the hell. Most races are shorter than that these days, so maybe he'll go two and a half after all."

Then a couple of men in suits showed up. "Time," announced one of them, flashing his credentials, and the other opened the stall door, then stood aside as Jamie led Tyrone down the aisle and out of the barn. The colt pricked up his ears and looked around but didn't seem at all nervous. I didn't know what you wanted in an auction yearling, but you got nervous if the horse you'd bet on started sweating heavily on the way to the post. Tyrone was dry as a bone, which is more than I could say for the two guys in suits walking alongside him in the Kentucky sun.

I'd seen photos of prior auctions in Tony's magazines, but evidently they'd all been taken at evening sessions, when the rich and famous felt compelled to wear tuxes and designer gowns. But as I entered the pavilion and surveyed the audience, I couldn't tell the billionaires from the trainers and the press (well, with a very few exceptions).

I noticed they'd stuck a label on Tyrone's right flank. It read "203," and from that moment until the auction ended he was known and referred to only as "Hip 203" by both the auctioneer and in the catalog.

He was third in line. A filly went for what I was told was a disappointing quarter of a million, and then the colt just ahead of Tyrone was led into the ring. There were a couple of bids, but the auctioneer couldn't elicit anymore, and he announced that the colt hadn't met his reserve—something like four hundred thousand—and would be returned to his breeder.

It got me wondering if maybe everyone had been overestimating either Tyrone's value or the health of the economy. I didn't know what his reserve was, or even if he had one, but I had a feeling that Bigelow, his breeder and consignor, must be getting a little nervous as Jamie led him into the ring.

It turned out that I worried for nothing. The opening bid was a million and a quarter, and the auctioneer was up past two million in less than a minute. I could see half a dozen of the rich and famous whispering with their trainers and their bloodstock agents. Finally one white-haired gent nodded his head, the auctioneer announced that the bid was two and a quarter, and somehow they passed over two and a half and two and three-quarters in the next few seconds to land on three million.

No one raised their hands or gave any other indication that they were about to bid, and the auctioneer, no fool he, just relaxed and gave them all another minute to confer. Then he announced, "Going once, going twice" and got a three-and-a-quarter-million bid before he could reach "going three times."

He gave everyone another minute, and this time no one bid, and Tyrone—excuse me, Hip 203—was sold to Khalid Rahjan, an oil-rich sheikh from Dubai or the Emirates (I never knew the difference; to me it's all "the Middle East"). I checked to see who was shaking his hand. That's when I found out that Biff Wainwright was his trainer, and that meant I might actually get a chance to see Tyrone when he began his career, because unlike Bill Halwell, who was strictly a West Coast man except for the Triple Crown and the Breeders' Cup, Wainwright often ran his horses in the Midwest.

As Tyrone was led out of the ring, Ben Miller walked over to me.

"Okay, Eli, they've got their own security, so there's no need for you to stick around. Go on back to Cincinnati and pick up your fee from the office tomorrow morning."

"Thanks," I said. "I was afraid that I might catch something, being exposed to all this money."

"I assume that's your notion of a joke."

"Probably," I replied.

"I hope so," said Miller. "You may not know it, but Bill Striker could buy and sell a third of these people."

I thanked him for another reminder of what I hadn't achieved with my life and began walking to the exit when a middle-aged couple approached me. They weren't dressed like most of the bidders, but zillionaires are allowed to be eccentric, so I came to a stop until they were standing in front of me.

"You're Mr. Paxton?" said the man.

"Eli," I replied.

He looked around uncomfortably. "We'd like to speak with you, but it's very crowded and noisy in here. Could we talk outside?"

"Lead the way," I said and fell into step behind them.

Once we were outside they stopped and turned to me.

"I am Marcus Sanders and this is my wife, Muriel."

Something about his name sounded familiar, but I couldn't place it, so I looked at him expectantly.

"We're Tony's parents."

"Tony the groom?"

"Yes."

"How is he?" I said. "I've been worried about him."

"So are we," said Marcus Sanders. "Mr. Bigelow phoned to tell us he'd run off and deserted the horse he was caring for, and that he would never work in this industry again."

"Do you know where he went?" I asked.

He shook his head. "He phoned us last night and said he wanted to talk to us, that something was bothering him and he'd be by in an hour."

"But he never showed up," said Mrs. Bigelow.

"Has he got a girlfriend?" I asked. "Maybe he's with her."

It was her turn to shake her head. "They broke up when he spent more time with the horses than with her. I don't think he's seen her in half a year."

"Besides," added Sanders, "that wouldn't be something he'd want to discuss with us."

"A lot of kids run off to California," I said. "Or these days, I think Denver and South Beach are two more prime destinations."

"He's never been as far from home as Nashville or Dayton, Mr. Paxton. He didn't drink and he didn't drug."

"You're sure?" I asked.

"He's our son," said Mrs. Sanders firmly. I hated to tell her how many parents said those same words while their kids were high as kites. She turned to her husband. "Tell him, Marcus."

"He seemed to like you," said Sanders. "At least he said so on the phone. And he said you were a detective." He paused. "We want to hire you to find our son."

"If he's skipped town, it could be weeks, even months," I told him.

"He hasn't left town," replied Sanders adamantly. "He wouldn't know where to go." He stared into my eyes. "He was worried, Mr. Paxton. He was coming home to talk about something, something important."

"And you've no idea what it was?"

"No. Have you?"

I shook my head. "He was happy as a lark when I went off to dinner and very upset when I came back. But that's all I know."

"Will you find him, Mr. Paxton?"

"No promises. I can look for him, but this is a town and an industry where I'm a total outsider."

"He trusted you," persisted Sanders.

"All right," I said. "I'm not the most expensive detective around here"—an understatement by a few hundred percent—"but no detective is cheap." I studied them, their clothes, their bearing, making my estimate. "My fee is a hundred and a half a day plus expenses, and a ten percent bonus if I find him. And I'll want five hundred as a retainer."

If he looked like he might back off, I was prepared to tell him I'd waive the retainer and the bonus because I was so fond of Tony, but instead he pulled out a checkbook, wrote "five hundred dollars" on a check that already had my name and the current date on it, and gave me a card with their address and phone number. Then he reached into a vest pocket and withdrew a folded sheet of paper, which he handed to me.

"A list of his friends," Sanders told me.

I studied it. "He didn't have too many, did he?"

"He was devoted to his work."

I nodded. "Yeah, that's the way he seemed to me."

"We trust you, Mr. Paxton," he said. "Find our son for us."

"And keep in touch," added his wife.

Then they were walking toward the parking lot, and I realized that I wasn't going home just yet.

5.

It was still an hour before dinnertime, and I figured since I was charging them for today I might as well get to work.

I wandered over to my car, stopped at the gate while track security made sure I wasn't hiding a valuable thoroughbred in the back of the Ford, then made my way to the nearest of the addresses the Sanderses had given me, which was a Jeff Calhoun.

It turned out to be an apartment building no more than two miles from the racetrack. I parked, walked in the front door, studied the mailboxes for a moment, finally found his name—he was sharing the place with two other guys—and rang the bell. Someone rang back, unlocking the inner door, and I entered, then began climbing to the third floor. A thin, ascetic-looking young man with a sparse mustache and sparser beard, wearing a T-shirt, blue jeans, and sandals, greeted me and ushered me in.

"Are you Jeff?" I asked as he led me into a living room that was even more beat-up and out of date than my own.

"No," he said. "I'm Spike. I'll get him for you."

I watched him as he walked down a corridor and knocked on a bedroom door, and wondered how anyone kept a straight face when they heard his name.

A burly, dark-haired guy, maybe twenty-five, with glasses and a mustache emerged and walked to the living room.

"You wanted to see me?" he said.

"Yeah," I began, starting to get up.

"Stay seated," he said, sitting in a chair opposite me. "We're informal here." A grin. "In fact, informal is probably an understatement. Now, what can I do for you, Mr. . . . ?"

"Paxton," I said. "Eli Paxton. I'm a private detective."

"Oh, hell!" he muttered. "Has Spike been smoking shit again?"

"I couldn't care less," I said with a reassuring smile. "I'm here about Tony Sanders."

He frowned. "Tony?" he repeated. "He's a sweet kid, even if he does prefer horses to people. What the hell has he done?"

"He's gone missing, and you're on a list of friends his parents gave me," I said. "When's the last time you saw him?"

"Probably not since he went to work for Bigelow," answered Calhoun.

"When was that?"

He shrugged. "Maybe a month ago. I used to see him a couple of times a week, but Mill Creek—that's Bigelow's farm—is a couple of miles out. Tony doesn't own a car, and I don't think any buses stop anywhere near it after dark."

"Was he happy there?" I asked.

"He was happy anywhere he could be near horses—well, near thoroughbreds, anyway. He didn't have any use for standardbreds."

"I'm a bit of a newcomer to the backstage part of racing," I said. "Can you tell me the difference?"

"Standardbreds are trotters," answered Calhoun. "I know they look alike, but it's like a whole different union."

"Got it," I said. "Did he ever give you any reason to think he was unhappy?"

"No, he loved his work. He wanted to be a trainer someday, but for the time being he was happy rubbing down quality thoroughbreds."

"Where had he been working, and why did he move to Bigelow's farm?"

"Grooms move around a lot," answered Calhoun. "They make it sound like they're experts, but really, how the hell much skill does it take to feed a horse or rub him down or muck out his stall? These farms with the million-dollar stallions, they don't just have vets on call; a lot of them have vets working right there on the grounds. So if the horse he's rubbing gets sick or hurt, no one expects him to do anything but report it pronto."

"So he didn't move to Bigelow's just to rub this colt that got sold earlier today?"

He shrugged again. "That might have had something to do with it. I mean, the colt was worth more and rubbing it probably brought more prestige than what he'd been rubbing over at Tilly Halstrom's farm. But my guess is that they paid him more money, or maybe Tilly's daughter made one too many plays for him. She's pretty well-known for that."

"And you haven't seen him in a month?"

"Well, about a month. Ever since he went to work for Mr. Bigelow."

I pulled the Sanderses' list out of my pocket and handed it to him. "You think any of these other guys might have seen him more recently?"

"Not if they didn't work there, and none of them did," he answered. Then he frowned. "Where the hell is Nan?"

"Beats me," I said. "Nan who?"

"Gillette. Tony's girl."

"His mother says they broke up half a year ago."

Jeff smiled. "She wanted them to break up, so Tony just stopped talking about her. He was still seeing her as of four or five days ago."

I frowned. "I thought you hadn't had any contact with him in a month."

"I haven't," he said. "But I see her all the time. She works at Fishbein's."

"Fishbein's?" I repeated.

"A drugstore about half a mile from here."

"You got a phone number or an address for her?"

He shook his head. "No, but she'll be working now. She pretty much arranged her hours so she'd be free late at night, when Tony could sneak away."

"Okay, where is this joint?"

"Out the front door, right for two blocks, then left for three. You can't miss it. Only drugstore within miles that's not Walgreen's or CVS."

"What's 'Nan' short for?"

He shrugged. "Beats the hell out of me. All I've ever called her is Nan. She and Tony and I were in the same high school class together. Well, until Tony and I quit, anyway."

"Okay," I said, getting to my feet. "Thanks for the information."

"Happy to help," he said, walking me to the door. "And if she's not there, maybe she and Tony finally got out of this town."

"You're not thrilled with Lexington?"

"It's a two-horse town," he answered. "One runs around the track, the other runs up and down the court at Rupp Arena."

I decided he probably wasn't far from right, thanked him again, and walked down the stairs. I went out to the Ford, started it up, and began making my way to Fishbein's. I had the radio on, but it was too early for the Reds, and all I got was a list of high-priced yearlings and their sires, as if their mothers had nothing to do with it.

It took about five minutes to get to Fishbein's—I was driving slowly and making sure I counted off the blocks correctly—and when I got there I found they had a lot on the side of the building, so I pulled in there, locked the car (not that there was anything worth stealing except the three packs of cigarettes I had hidden in the glove compartment in case I fell off that particular wagon), and entered the store.

It was almost empty, just a couple of old ladies arguing with the pharmacist that generics shouldn't cost more than a dollar apiece, and I walked around until I saw a pretty young blonde, maybe eighteen or nineteen years old, straightening some shelves.

"Good afternoon," I said, approaching her.

She flashed me an insincere smile and went back to what she was doing.

"I wonder if you can help me," I continued. "I'm looking for a young lady named Nan."

She stared at me but said nothing.

I pulled out my detective's license—most people can't tell it from a badge—and said, "I just want to talk to her. No laws have been broken and no arrests will be made."

"I'm Nan," she said, "Nanette, actually."

I figured it was probably Nancy and that she decided Nanette sounded classier. Made no difference to me, so I didn't comment on it.

"Hi, Nan," I said. "My name is Eli Paxton. I'm a private detective—"

"I've never seen one before, except on television," she replied. "Do you carry a gun?"

"Rarely and carefully," I answered.

"What do you want from me?" she asked, suddenly apprehensive.

"Just some information about a young man named Tony Sanders."

"Oh, my God!" she gasped. "What did he do?"

"Disappeared."

She frowned. "What do you mean?"

"I mean that last night he was guarding this colt that was up for sale today, and this morning he was missing and no one can find him."

"And you think *I'm* hiding him?"

I shrugged. "What would you be hiding him from?"

"Nothing."

"Have you any idea why he might have walked away from his job on what figured to be both its most important and its final day?"

She shook her head.

"Has he mentioned anything to you, anything that might be troubling him?"

She shook her head again. "He was very happy. We were going out tomorrow night." She frowned again. "It better not be another girl!"

"I doubt it," I said. "I spoke to him last night and he seemed very disturbed about something. Do you have any idea what it might have been?"

"No."

"Has he ever mentioned a desire to see other places?" I continued. "Maybe California, maybe, I don't know, Miami?"

"Tony?" she said incredulously. "I don't think he's ever been thirty miles from here. Whenever we've talked about getting married and going on a honeymoon, the farthest he would even consider is Mammoth Cave."

I pulled a card out of my wallet, then realized that I was a hundred miles from the phone, and scribbled the Hyatt's number on the back of it, then handed it to her.

"If you should hear from him, call this number and leave a message for Ben Miller. He'll see to it that I get it."

"Why don't I just call you on your cell phone?" she asked.

"It's broken," I lied. "And I haven't had a chance to pick up a new one."

"You could buy one right here," she said. "We're running a sale."

"My company's picking one up for me," I said, which was easier than explaining that I refused to own a cell phone or even learn how they worked.

"Well, when you get a number, call here and leave it for me."

"Will do," I said.

"Damn, I hope he's all right."

"He's probably fine," I said. "Young men just tend to get restless." It didn't sound all that reasonable even to me, and I could tell she wasn't buying it. "I'll keep in touch," I promised her and headed out the door.

I tried the other three friends on the list. Two were out, and the third had nothing to add. Tony loved horses and the racing game, he had eyes for no two-legged female except Nan, and he seemed happy as a clam the last time they'd met.

By the time I was through hitting all the addresses and talking to the last friend, it was nearing nine o'clock, and I realized I hadn't eaten dinner yet, so I stopped at a Bob Evans, had some steak and eggs and a piece of pecan pie, downed a couple of cups of coffee, and hunted up a Motel 6, which cost about as much as a closet in the downtown Hyatt. I left a message for Ben Miller, telling him where he could find me if he had to, took a shower, and got ready for bed.

About two in the morning my phone rang. I picked it up, grunted a "Hello" into it, and was rewarded by the sound of Ben Miller's voice.

"Eli, this is Ben. Sorry to wake you, but I just got in."

"What's up?"

"Message for you from someone called Nanette. Says to call her, night or day." He gave me the number.

"Thanks, Ben."

"You working on that missing groom?"

"Yeah."

"Good luck."

He hung up, and I dialed Nan's number.

"Yes?" said a wide-awake female voice.

"Hi, Nan. This is Eli Paxton."

"Thank goodness!" she said.

"You've heard from him?"

"No," she replied. "But I lied to you before. Now that I've had time to think about it, I realize I should have told you the truth. I thought I was protecting him, but you're being paid to find and protect him too."

"Okay," I said. "What can you tell me?"

"I did hear from him last night."

"When?"

"Just before midnight," she said. "He sounded very upset, very worried. He wouldn't say what it was, but he said he had to come by and talk to me in person, either today or tomorrow . . . well, yesterday or today, now."

"Did he give you any hint of what was bothering him?"

"No. Just that he had to do or see something, and then we'd talk."

"Nothing about any of the owners or trainers, at the track or at the farm?" I persisted. "Nothing he heard them say? I mean, a lot of them are filthy rich, and I'm sure their dealings aren't always ethical or legal."

"No, not a word about it."

"Did you get the feeling he thought he was in danger?"

"Just worried."

"What kind of things worried him?"

"I don't know!" she said in an exasperated tone, and a few seconds later she was crying.

"Calm down," I said. "Thank you for the information."

"And you're not mad at me for lying?"

"I'm grateful to you for finally telling the truth."

"And you'll let me know when you find him and that he's all right?"

"Yes."

She hung up without another word.

I thought about it for a while, realized there was nothing to be done at two-fifteen in the morning, and lay back on the bed. I'd run through Tony's friends, so I decided that, come sunrise, I'd pay a visit to Bigelow's farm.

6.

Mill Creek Farm was about fifteen miles out of town. It wasn't one of the classic farms like Claiborne or Calumet or Gainesway, but over the years Travis Bigelow had produced his share of stakes winners. No Derby winners, but that seemed to be a lot more important to sportswriters who followed racing two or three days a year than to the people in the industry.

I kept looking for blue grass, and what I kept seeing was green grass. I drove past a few thoroughbred farms with picturesque white split-rail fences for the public and electric wires that delivered a very mild shock for the horses, since some of the more athletic horses could probably jump the fence, but they couldn't jump the electric wire that ran along the top of it maybe a foot or so above the top rail.

A number of the farms had training tracks, but no one was out running on them as I drove past. What struck me was the size of the pastures. You could stick a hundred head of cattle into each enclosed pasture that housed from one to ten thoroughbreds. Then I thought about it and realized that it made sense, that based on some of the figures Tony had quoted, there was every likelihood that one top race-horse or stallion was worth more than a hundred cows.

Finally I came to a sign telling me I'd reached Mill Creek Farm. I turned into the driveway, which was lined with fenced pastures on both sides, and started driving up to the house. There were a quartet of barns off to the left, and another to the right. Straight ahead was what I assumed was a typical horse country mansion, a large two-story white house with a quartet of huge white pillars holding up a portico in the front.

There was actually a uniformed guy standing at the front door. He walked over when I pulled up and waited for me to open the window.

"May I help you, sir?" he asked.

"I hope so," I said. "My name's Eli Paxton. I'd like to talk to the guy who does the hiring around here, or if he's at the sale, then to Mr. Bigelow."

"I'm afraid we are not currently hiring," said the man.

I pulled out my wallet and flashed my license at him. "I'm not looking for work. I'm here about a missing groom."

He sighed deeply. "They come and go all the time, sir."

"Just the same, I'd like to talk to someone who knew him, and maybe take a look around."

He frowned. "Mr. Standish is the farm manager. I believe he's in one of the barns. As for letting you 'look around'"—I could almost hear the quote marks around it—"you will require Mr. Bigelow's permission."

"Is he home?"

"He will be shortly. I believe he's at the bank."

I couldn't blame him. If I had a check for three and a quarter million in my pocket, I'd want to make sure it was good too.

"Well, if you'll point out where this Standish is, I can start by talking to him."

"I can't leave my post, sir. I'll summon someone to take you to him."

He pulled out a cell phone that made Star Trek's communicators look like primitive kid stuff, spoke into it so softly I couldn't hear him, and then tucked it away.

"Well?" I asked.

He pointed to a young man who was walking toward us from the nearest barn.

"This is Jeremy," he said. "He will take you to Mr. Standish."

"Has he got a first name?"

"I just told you."

"I mean Standish," I said.

"Frank."

"Okay, thanks," I said, but he was already walking back to his station at the front door.

I decided that since he hadn't told me to move the car, I'd leave it right where it was so I could find it again when I was done. I got out, closed the door, wished I had one of those remote control locks—not that there was anything worth stealing, but just because I didn't want anyone pushing the car out of the way—and began walking across the lush green field toward Jeremy.

We met halfway between the barn and the house, introduced ourselves, and shook hands.

"Hector tells me you're a cop?" he said.

"Hector?" I repeated. "No wonder he didn't tell me his name."

Jeremy chuckled. "I read about a Hector in high school. Some Greek guy. Got himself killed by another Greek guy." We began walking toward the farthest barn. "So what's a cop doing here?"

"I'm a private eye," I said.

"Wow!" he said excitedly. "I've never met one of them before! You got an office and a sexy secretary and girls stashed all over the city like all those private dicks on television?"

"Well, I have an office, anyway," I said.

"So what are you here for?"

"A groom's gone missing, and I've been hired to find him."

"Another?"

"This has happened before?"

"Happens all the time. The old grooms, they don't know nothing else so they stick around forever, but the young guys like me, we're just passing through. Who's flown the coop?"

"You know Tony Sanders?"

"Tony? Sure." Jeremy frowned. "But he's the last guy I'd expect to walk away. He loved horses and racing. I mean, every time someone would talk about heading off to California or maybe Miami, all he could talk about was Santa Anita and Hialeah."

I nodded my head. "That's Tony, all right."

"What's running this week?" said Jeremy, frowning. "Arlington, I think. And Belmont. Probably Monmouth. Oh. And Hollywood or Del Mar, something out west. You want him, that's where you'll find him. He probably hooked up with some trainer, talked himself into a job while they were all looking at Tyrone."

"I don't know," I said. "He seemed pretty upset last night."

"Have you met Nan?"

"Yeah."

Jeremy smiled. "If you were leaving a looker like her, wouldn't you be upset?"

It sounded logical, but it felt wrong. Something more than leaving his girlfriend behind had been bothering him.

"Maybe you're right," I said, "but I need to talk to Mr. Standish and probably Mr. Bigelow, just to be thorough."

"Call him Frank," said Jeremy. "Everyone does."

"Gotcha."

"He could have been a hell of a trainer," continued Jeremy. "In fact, he was once." He shook his head. "Too bad."

"What happened?" I asked.

"He won some big filly-and-mare stakes race out east, the winner flunked her drug test, and he was ruled off for a year, so he took a job managing the Wilson farm a few miles south of here, and then when the job opened up here a few months ago, he took it." He frowned again. "You know the crazy part? They busted up some doping ring a couple of years later, and one of them admitted he'd doped Frank's filly. But by then he'd settled in and was raising a family and didn't want to go back on the circuit. I asked him about it a couple of times, if he missed it. He said that sometimes he did, but racing's not like football or basketball or any other sport: it's twelve months a year, and he didn't want to be away from his wife and kids all the time."

"Makes sense," I said.

"You away from your wife much?"

"Constantly," I said.

He looked puzzled.

"We're divorced."

"Hell, just about everybody is these days. Well, except for Frank and Mr. Bigelow. And if he got rid of that witch, we'd all cheer."

"Frank's wife?" I asked.

He laughed. "No, Mrs. Bigelow. She always goes around acting like she's too good for us common folks—but it's us common folks who run her goddamned farm for her."

We reached the largest barn, and Jeremy escorted me inside, where a middle-aged man was on his knees, running his hands over a horse's ankle while a female groom held its halter.

"Yeah, there's definitely some heat there," he said to the girl. "Keep him in his stall. I'll check every morning, and if it's still there in two days we'll get the vet in here."

"I thought all the big farms had vets in residence," I said.

"Not when they're dispersing all their stock," he said, standing up as she led the horse away. He turned to look at me. "Should I know you?"

I extended my hand. "My name's Eli Paxton. I'd like to ask you a couple of questions."

He shook his head. "Pleased to meet you, Mr. Paxton, but anything you want to know about what's for sale, you'll have to talk to Mr. Bigelow."

"I'm not here to buy a horse," I answered. "I'm a private detective, working on a missing person case."

"Who's missing?"

"A young man named Tony Sanders."

"Yeah, I heard about that," answered Standish. "Mr. Bigelow was fit to be tied, walking off when he had a three-million-dollar yearling in his care."

"I spent a little time with him before he went missing," I said. "He seemed like a nice, responsible kid."

"He was," agreed Standish. "Or at least I thought so until I heard he'd taken off. I was actually thinking of getting him work with Milt Baynes in another year or so."

"Milt Baynes?" I repeated.

"A local trainer. Mostly claimers and cheap allowance horses, but at least the kid could get the feel of the business." He shook his head. "Well, they come and they go. He'd only been here a month. You'd think rubbing down a horse like Tyrone would keep them happy." He shrugged. "Who understands kids these days?"

"You said 'them'?" I asked.

"Yeah," answered Standish. "I hired Tony because the kid who was rubbing Tyrone took a powder one night. Probably busy turning his brain to porridge in some crack house."

"What was the kid's name?" I asked.

"There's no connection," Standish assured me. "They didn't even know each other. One flew the coop, and I hired the other two days later, once I was sure he wasn't coming back."

"Oh, I'm sure there's no direct connection," I replied. "But maybe the grooms have a grapevine. You know: go to such-and-so a place for the best pot or the friendliest women, that kind of thing. I assume no one's hired any detective to hunt for the first groom, so if I can turn up any information on him, it might lead me to Tony."

"Sounds like a long shot to me," said Standish. "But hell, this is one business where long shots do come in. Kid's name was Billy something... give me a sec." He lowered his head in thought, then looked up. "Billy Paulson, I think. Tell you what: leave me your card and I'll hunt up his job application when I'm through making my rounds and have one of the kids drive it over to you."

I pulled a card out and scribbled the motel's address on it, then handed it to him.

"Thanks, Frank."

"My pleasure," he said. "If you find where all the runaway grooms from this town are hiding, you're gonna need a baseball stadium to hold 'em all. I mean, it's hardly permanent work, even with a horse like Tyrone."

"He was a nice-looking horse to my unpracticed eye," I said.

"You don't sell for three mil if you've got a case of the uglies," said Standish. "I remember his papa as a youngster, and just between you and me and the gatepost, Tyrone was a much better-looking animal, even with that scar on his neck. I gather he got it a few weeks before I arrived; it was still healing when I got here."

"I'm surprised the breeder didn't have an urge to keep him and race him," I remarked.

"You mean Mr. Bigelow?" asked Standish.

I nodded.

"He hasn't raced in, oh, it must be fifteen years. In fact, he's just about through breeding. Sold his interest in Trojan and a couple of other stallions, and has sold a batch of his broodmares privately."

"So he's getting out of it?"

"He'd better be," replied Standish. "You don't see it up front, but the working part of this farm needs close to half a million worth of repairs and upgrades, and who the hell knows what the house needs? I think the missus has been after him to leave the Blue Grass and go back to civilization in some high-rise for a couple of years now." He paused and sighed deeply. "Still, there was a time, and not so long ago, when this place was one of the crown jewels." He shrugged. "I guess everything changes. Doesn't mean we have to like it."

"Does Mr. Bigelow know the hired help?" I asked. "I mean personally?"

"He knows the long-timers, of course. As for the grooms and the groundskeepers, he knows most of 'em by sight, and knows a few of their names," answered Standish. "But he's been in town all week, with his lawyers and his bankers and whoever the hell else he has to see during sales week. He won't be able to tell you anything."

"I believe you," I said. "But I might as well speak to him as long as I'm here, just to please my clients."

"Tony's parents?"

"Right."

"I never met them, but he seemed to think well of them. I hope you run the kid down before he gets in any serious trouble."

"Hell, I just hope he's not in any yet," I said.

"I'm with you on that. Nice kid. Had a way with horses." He began walking to the barn door. "Come on. I'll take you up to the big house and introduce you. Watch your step near the door. Got a busted pipe there. Jury-rigged a patch on it until we can get a plumber out here."

I walked around the pipe and followed him outside. A big earth-moving machine was parked about forty feet from the entrance.

"The place needs a lot of repairs," confided Standish. "We think there's also a leak in the main line leading from the street."

"That's a lot of ground to dig up," I said, turning and looking toward the street.

"True," he agreed. "On the other hand," he added with a smile, "we have a lot of horses who like to drink."

As we walked by one of the barns I saw a quartet of monuments, statues of horses with inscriptions on them.

"What's that?" I asked.

"The cemetery," he replied.

"You've only had four horses die in all the years this place has been here?" I asked with a smile.

He returned the smile. "Most are disposed of by the vet. But these four deserved to be remembered. All the farms do it. Go by Claiborne and you can pay your respects to Secretariat, Bold Ruler, and Danzig. Stop by Calumet and you can do the same to Citation and Alydar and some others." He paused. "What we have here are Vanguard, Gunslinger, Midnight Run, and Silk Scarf."

"Silk Scarf?" I repeated. "Wasn't that a filly?"

He nodded. "A mare. They're colts and fillies until they turn five; then they're horses and mares. She just died this spring."

"Isn't it odd for a mare to be buried here? Every horse you named here and at the other farms were males."

"She produced eight stakes winners," said Standish. "That's more than some males produce with fifty times the offspring." Another pause. "Hell, Ruffian is buried at Belmont Park, and when Zenyatta goes she'll have a marker that dwarfs all of these."

"I wonder what kind of grave is in store for Tyrone, if any," I mused as we continued walking.

"First let's see if he can beat you at even weights," said Standish with a smile. "Then we'll worry about ranking him with racing's immortals."

"Don't you have some idea by now?" I asked.

"Some," he replied. "But I just got here myself a few months ago. I haven't really watched him develop from the start. He seems like a well-balanced colt, good shoulder, good muscle, and well bred."

"But?" I prompted him.

"But a lot of well-balanced, well-bred colts wind up running in claiming races."

"Yeah," I said. "Whenever I'm at the track, I never bet the best-bred horse in a claiming race. I figure if his owner's willing to sell him for a few thousand bucks, and his daddy's stud fee is up there in the stratosphere, someone has a good reason for dumping him, and that gives me just as good a reason for not betting him."

"I've never heard it put quite that way, but it makes sense," said Frank.

We reached the house—my urge is to call it the mansion, or at least the big house—in a couple of minutes. Hector opened the door for us, stepped aside as we passed through, and closed it behind us.

The house had been as elegant as a palace once, I could see that at a glance. But the more I looked, the more I saw that the place had fallen on hard times. The carpeting was almost as threadbare as my own, and it didn't have the excuse of Marlowe trying to bury his bones under it. The couches and chairs had seen better days, and there was even some wallpaper peeling off the wall.

It was clear that Jeremy was right: the Bigelows had to be planning on selling out and moving away. Not just because they were dispersing their horses, but because no one who dealt in million-dollar horseflesh would live like this unless they were about to unload the place.

"We'll go to the study," said Standish, turning and leading me to a smaller room just as shabby as the others. "This is where he likes to talk business." We sat on a very uncomfortable couch that had seen better days but probably no more comfortable ones and stared at an empty chair and desk.

After a couple of minutes Travis Bigelow entered the room. He was a dapper-looking man in his sixties or seventies, with thinning white hair, a thick mustache, a fancy cane he carried but didn't seem to need, and a dark three-piece suit with a muted tie.

"Hector told me you'd brought a visitor, Frank," he said, staring at me.

"Right," said Standish, getting to his feet, and I followed suit. "This is Eli Paxton."

Bigelow stared at me. "I don't believe we've met, Mr. Paxton."

"We don't travel in the same circles," I said with a smile. "I'm a private detective."

He frowned. "Another goddamned lawsuit?"

"No, sir," I said. "This has nothing to do with you. Or only marginally. A groom who worked for you is missing, and I've been hired to find him."

"Oh, good," he said. "I didn't mean to be rude or suspicious, Mr. Paxton. But when you're as rich as I am, you get the damnedest demands from people who want to grab a piece of what you've got, and usually a detective or a lawyer is a harbinger of things to come."

"I understand, sir," I said. I decided not to add that I hoped he kept it all in cash and tax-frees, because the house and barns looked a lot worse from the inside than the outside.

"So who is this missing groom?" said Bigelow.

"A young man named Tony Sanders," I said.

"Sanders, Sanders," he said. "Are you quite sure? I don't think I know the name."

"He'd only been here a month," I said.

He shrugged. "You can't expect me to know every kid who passes through here."

"No, I can't," I agreed. "But since he was in charge of your three-million-dollar yearling..."

"Nonsense!" he snapped. "Frank was in charge of him. Tony just fed and cleaned him."

"Then you do know him," I said.

"I don't know him," he replied adamantly. "You already told me his name was Tony and that he was Tyrone's groom." He paused. "I wish his new owner well. That's a hell of a horse. Almost makes me wish I was still racing them."

"I got the impression you never raced your own horses, sir," I said.

"I got into this decades ago with some cheap claiming horses," he replied. "Even moved one of them up to stakes competition. It was when I learned where the real money was that I gave it up to be a market breeder. I hope to hell Tyrone goes out and wins some major races for his new owner . . . but if he doesn't, I've still got my three and a quarter million."

"Makes sense to me," I said, and then paused for a moment. "Now, getting back to Tony . . ."

"Like I said, I don't know the young man, but far be it from me to hinder you in the pursuit of justice or truth or whatever the hell it is you're pursuing."

"Right now what I'm pursuing is Tony Sanders," I said.

"Okay, Mr. Packard . . ."

"Paxton," I corrected him.

"Mr. Paxton," he said. "You have free run of the farm. Frank, he can look anywhere he wants, interview anyone he wants." He turned to me. "Will that be satisfactory?"

"I couldn't ask for anything more," I replied. Well, maybe your house and three and a quarter million, but what the hell.

"Then I think our conversation is over," he said, extending his hand. "It was very nice to meet you, Mr. Paxton, and I hope you find the young man."

"Eli, go on out," said Standish. "I'll join you in just a minute."

I left the study and began walking to the front door. They closed the study door, but it was warped along the top, and I could hear Standish's voice saying, "Are we going to get our paychecks today, sir?"

"Yes," said Bigelow. "I'll have Marvin write them out and deliver them this afternoon. I'm sorry, Frank; he and I were both tied up all day at the bank."

I couldn't hear anything further without coming to a complete stop, and Hector the guard was standing by the open front door staring at me, so I went outside and waited for Standish there.

As I tripped over a loose brick in the doorway, I found myself thinking that if Tony had had any money, I could well believe Bigelow had murdered him for it, just to help repair the once-proud and now-dilapidated Mill Creek Farm.

7.

I spent an hour nosing around the barns, escorted by Frank Standish. I spoke to some of the grooms and the other hired help. Everyone liked Tony, no one had a bad word to say about him, and no one was surprised that he had left. Kids were doing that all the time, and even at nineteen or twenty he was still a kid in this industry.

I figured the next stop was the local police station. I hate cooling my heels while the cops check my credentials at their usual snail's pace, so I called ahead, gave them my name, told them to check with Jim Simmons of the Cincinnati police, then went out for lunch (or maybe it was a late breakfast, since I hadn't eaten since I got up), smoked a cigarette when my conscience wasn't looking, and finally drove over to the station.

I introduced myself to the desk clerk (or maybe she was the desk clerkess, a redhead in her forties), and she led me to the office I wanted. A uniformed cop sat behind a desk, and when I entered he stood up and extended his hand.

"Lou Berger," he said.

"And I'm Eli Paxton," I replied, taking his hand.

"Jim Simmons has nice things to say about you," said Berger. "Have a seat and tell me what's on your mind."

"I'm trying to track down a young man who went missing yesterday," I said, sitting down opposite him.

"Just since yesterday?" he said, frowning. "That hardly qualifies as missing. Has he got a girl or maybe a habit?"

I shook my head. "His girl hasn't seen him, and no one's ever seen him smoking, snorting, or shooting any junk."

"Still, one day . . ." he said dubiously.

"The circumstances were unusual," I told him.

"In what way?"

"Did you read or hear about that Trojan colt who went for over three million yesterday?"

"A little out of my league, but, yeah, you can't live in this town and not hear about the yearling sales."

"Well, this kid was his groom."

"And he just walked off the job?" said Berger. "He's gonna have a hard time finding work in that industry when he finally shows up."

"There's a little more to it than that," I continued.

Suddenly he looked alert. "Tell me," he said.

"I was hired as security for the horse."

"You one of Bill Striker's men?"

"Temporarily," I said. "Anyway, the night before the auction something happened."

"What?"

I shook my head. "Damned if I know. But this was a friendly, happy, carefree kid when I went out for dinner, and when I came back he looked worried and maybe a little bit scared. I asked what was wrong, and he told me he had to think about it, that maybe he'd tell me in the morning."

"And did he?"

I shook my head. "I went to bed, and as far as I know, no one's seen him since."

"You doing this for Striker?"

"No, for the kid's parents."

He nodded. "Makes sense. I can't imagine the Striker Agency would be interested, or that anyone connected with a groom could afford them." He pulled out a pen and a pad of paper. "Okay, Eli, what's his name?"

"Tony Sanders," I said. "I can get you a photo of him from his parents."

"Not a bad idea," said Berger. "I'll ask around and put it out on the wire, but I wouldn't hold my breath. Kids run away all the time, and shoveling horseshit isn't the kind of job you fight to keep hold of."

"I know. If I hadn't spent a couple of days with him, I'd figure he was hitching his way to California."

"These days it's Florida," replied Berger. "Say Florida and everyone thinks about the Mouse, but go down to South Beach and there is every stimulant you could want, including a few thousand dead-gorgeous topless girls out on the sand. That's where they run to, at least from the Midwest."

"Anyway, thanks for your time and trouble," I said, getting to my feet. "I'll check in every day or two."

"My pleasure, Eli. Where are you staying?"

I gave him my hotel's phone number. "Anything happens, just leave a message for me to call you."

"Will do," he said. "Nice meeting you."

"Same here," I said, reaching for the door. Suddenly I froze.

"Is something wrong?" he asked.

"This is probably nothing, but Tony had been with Mill Creek and the Trojan colt for only about a month. He replaced another groom who just up and vanished one day. I wonder if you've got anything on him?"

"You think there's a connection?"

"Probably not," I said. "Hell, almost certainly not. But since I'm not likely to be sent to South Beach . . ."

He smiled. "Okay. What's his name?"

"Billy Paulson," I said, and then added, "Probably."

"He wasn't sure or you're not sure?"

"Frank Standish wasn't sure. He's supposed to be checking for me."

"Hell, I know Frank. We bowl in the same league. I'll call him myself and ask."

"Thanks," I said, opening the door. "And this time I will leave."

"By the way," he said, "it's a two-way street. I'll share anything I can get on either kid, but you'll do the same. We don't need any more heroes."

"Not a problem," I said. "Hell, I used to be a cop. I've never considered you guys enemies or rivals, and I'll bet every last one of you goes to the shooting range and the gym more than I do, even the redhead who ushered me in."

"You want to see tough?" he asked with a grin. "Her name's Bernice. Pinch her bottom and see what happens."

"I'll take your word for it," I said.

"You'll live longer if you do."

Then I walked out of his office and the building, wondering what the hell else I could do to earn my money.

8.

I went back to Keeneland, planning to ask some of the other grooms, or even the uniformed guards, if Tony had said anything to them that might give a hint as to what was bothering him. I knew the odds were that he was off with a bottle or a bimbo or both, but I couldn't help remembering how worried he was the last time I saw him—and it wasn't just me. Nanette had sensed the same thing.

He was going to talk to her in the morning when he'd settled his problem, or at least figured out what to do about it, and he'd said pretty much the same thing to me.

So my first question, of course, was what was his problem?

That led to a second question: he hardly knew me, but why couldn't he talk to Nan, or even his parents, about it?

And that led to the third question: he'd been fine when I went off to dinner, and an hour later he was as troubled as any kid I've ever seen, and the next morning he was gone without a trace. What the hell had happened during that hour?

I hunted up the guard who had originally led me to Barn 9. He was standing just inside the aisle to Barn 7, looking pretty relaxed now that about three-quarters of the yearlings had been sold and taken to their new homes, and there was a lot less hustle and bustle.

"Ah, Mr. Paxton," he said as I approached him. "How may I help you?"

"Start by staying in the shade and let me join you," I said. "That sun's a bitch."

"That it is, sir," he said as I stood next to him. He stared at me for a moment. "You're here about the young man who was rubbing the Trojan colt." It was a statement, not a question.

"Yeah, that's right."

"I heard he'd gone missing. Foolish timing, walking out the day his colt went up for sale." He shook his head. "I don't know who'll hire him now, and I do know that he loved the sport, studied it more than some of the trainers you see around here."

"Did he say anything to you the last day he was here?"

"He probably said 'Hi,'" replied the guard.

"Anything else?" I said. "Especially toward evening?"

He shook his head. "Not that I can recall."

"I spoke to him when I got back from dinner," I continued. "He was pretty worried about something. Distressed is the word I'd use."

"I don't think I saw him after late afternoon," was the reply. "The auction had already begun, and I was directing people to the sales pavilion most of the night."

"He was here when I went to bed, maybe eleven or midnight," I said, "and he was gone in the morning. Maybe the night shift can help."

"I'm sorry to disappoint you, Mr. Paxton, but there isn't a night shift."

"With all those trillions of dollars of horseflesh on the grounds?" I said, frowning.

"Maybe I should clarify that," he said. "Of course we have a night staff, but it's much smaller, since no owners or trainers are expected to be wandering the grounds. I think there are six men, total, and they're more concerned with vandals at the clubhouse and the sales pavilion than with the horses. I believe only two men are in charge of all the barns, and of course they won't enter one without a reason, because they don't want to upset the horses or wake those grooms who are staying here."

"Okay," I said with a sigh. "I'm just trying to cover all the angles."

"Are you working for his parents?"

"Yeah."

"Maybe you'd be willing to take something to them."

"What?" I asked.

"Even if he turns up, he's not going to be back in the barns here," answered the guard. "He left a couple dozen racing magazines here. If they're still here in a couple of days I'll just throw them out, so I thought you might take them in case you luck out and find him." He paused and shook his head again. "Even if you do, I don't think anyone'll hire him, certainly not until they all forget about this."

"What the hell," I said. "I might as well take them."

"Follow me," said the guard. He led me to Barn 9, and then to one of the tack rooms—not the one I'd slept in—and there, on a beat-up wood table, were maybe twenty magazines, the same ones I'd seen Tony reading during the past few days.

"Thanks," I said, lifting them up and starting to head out the door toward the parking lot.

"I hope you find him," said the guard. "He was a nice kid, one of the better ones."

"I liked him too."

"Can I ask you a question?" he said.

"Sure."

"Do you think he's run off, like so many other kids?"

"Seriously?" I said. "No. I can't forget how worried he was."

"If he didn't run away, what do you suppose happened to him?"

I shrugged. "Let's hope nothing did."

"Have you talked to the cops?"

I nodded. "Yeah. But it's really too early for them to have any reports on runaways who have been spotted."

"I didn't mean that."

I stared at him for a moment and finally understood. "If his body turns up, I'll know as soon as they identify him. And if they can't identify him, then they'll call me and his parents in, and we'll do it."

"You're sure?"

"Yeah."

"Well," he said as we reached the end of the row of barns and I headed for the parking lot, "good luck, Mr. Paxton."

"Thanks," I said. "I have a feeling I'm going to need it."

I got to the car, loaded the magazines into the trunk, and tried to figure out where to go next. Then I figured, what the hell, the track kitchen was right here, and maybe they'd think my meals were still being picked up by the Striker Agency.

I walked in the door, nodded to the guy behind the counter, sat down, picked up a discarded newspaper, and tried to find out how the Reds were doing. I finally got a score, buried beneath a dozen articles about the sale.

"What can I get for you—Eli, is it?" asked the counterman.

"A cheeseburger and a cup of coffee," I said.

"Coming right up."

"Got a minute?" I asked.

He looked around at the near-empty place and smiled. "Yeah, no one'll starve in the next sixty seconds."

"Did you know Tony Sanders?" I asked.

He shrugged. "Should I?"

"He was a groom."

"For one of the sales yearlings?" he said. "Hell, none of them were on the grounds for as much as a week."

"Well, it was worth a try."

"Who did he work for?"

"Mill Creek."

"That Bigelow guy?"

"Right."

"How's Frank Standish doing?" he asked. "Now, that was a trainer. Why the hell did he quit?"

"He decided his family was more important," I said.

"Families are a dime a dozen," he said. "But there's only one Trojan or Secretariat or Zenyatta."

"Well, if he felt like you, I imagine he'd be training horses on the Coast and wondering why his wife left him."

He chuckled at that. "Yeah, maybe you got a point. Especially if his wife looked like Jenny Piccolo."

"Jenny who?" I said, frowning.

"You haven't heard of her?"

"Nope."

"Poor bastard. She trains for a couple of big stables out West—and she also posed for some magazine's center spread. Talk about everything in one package! Too bad Frank didn't see her first."

"Your sympathy is heartwarming," I said. "Now how about my sandwich?"

He walked over to the grill and was back a few minutes later.

"I don't mean to be nosy," he said nosily, "but why the hell are you still here?"

"I'm looking for Tony Sanders."

"The groom. Wish I could help you."

"Let me try one more name out on you," I said.

"Shoot."

"Billy Paulson."

"Didn't he used to ride at Bowie or Delaware Park?"

I shook my head. "He's another groom."

"So two of them flew the coop during the sale? That's unusual."

"No, Paulson's been missing for a month."

"Who knows where the hell he's gotten to by now?" was the response.

"Oh, somebody must," I said.

"Lotsa luck," he said, and walked off to serve another customer.

Problem was, luck was in short supply—or at least it was until I pulled up to the Motel 6 lot and walked in the front entrance.

9.

I don't know why I walked into the lobby. I already had a room; all I had to do was park in front of it. I wasn't short of cigarettes or change, and they didn't sell beer. Just force of habit, I guess.

"Hi, Mr. Paxton," said the clerk. "Phone message for you. You can pick it up on your room's phone, or I can give it to you right here."

"I don't think I have any secrets worth hiding since I broke up with Pam Anderson last week," I said. "Let's have it."

He handed me a slip of paper he'd written on. His scrawl was so illegible that I couldn't make out a word of it.

"A Mr. Berger phoned and said to contact him, that he had some information for you." He shrugged. "I don't know what it could be. They haven't run at Keeneland since the end of April, and the sale ended a couple of hours ago."

He looked at me expectantly, as if I was supposed to confide in him.

"Paris Hilton's boyfriend," I said. "Jealous as hell."

"You private eyes do get around," he said.

"Yeah," I replied. "That's why we all stay at Motel 6's. Those jealous boyfriends never think to look for us here."

I went to my room, unlocked the door, stepped inside, and walked over to the phone. The message light was blinking, and I pressed it, then sat down to hear what Berger had to say.

"Hello, Eli? This is Lou Berger. It was a slow afternoon, so I had time to do a little checking in our files, and I found something I think might interest you. I'll be here 'til eight tonight, or give me a call tomorrow."

I checked my watch. It was a quarter to seven, and his office was no more than seven or eight minutes away, so I hopped back into the Ford and drove over to the police station.

Bernice the redhead gave me a welcoming smile as I entered.

"Welcome again," she said. "I assume you're here to see Officer Berger?"

I nodded. "That's right. I believe he's expecting me."

"I'll take you there," she said, starting to walk around the desk.

"It's not necessary, Bernice," I said. "I can find my own way."

"How did you know my name is Bernice?"

"You just look like a Bernice," I said.

"Oh?"

"Gorgeous, redheaded, not a hair out of place, not a button unbuttoned. What could it be but Bernice?"

She was still beaming when I walked down the hall and entered Lou Berger's room. He was on the phone. He smiled and waved to me, pointed to a chair, and finished up his conversation in maybe half a minute.

"Glad you could make it," he said. "I didn't really expect to see you until tomorrow."

"I got your call maybe ten minutes ago. It was nothing to drive over here before you're off-duty."

"Want some coffee?"

"Not right now," I said, leaning forward. "What have you got on Tony Sanders?"

"Not a damned thing."

"But your call said—"

"My call said I did a little digging and came up with something interesting," replied Berger. "And I did."

"So what is it?"

"The other groom you mentioned—Billy Paulson?"

"Yeah?"

"Seems he phoned us the day before he vanished," said Berger. "I was on vacation that week, but I found the records. He thought someone might want to kill him. We asked him who and why, and he said he didn't want to talk about it yet, that he might be wrong, but if he didn't call in every day to go looking for him."

"And?" I asked.

"Never heard from him again. Had a couple of officers spend a day or two looking for him, checking with friends, family, the farm. They finally concluded he just ran off for whatever reason, and there didn't seem to be anyone chasing him."

"And this was about a month ago?"

He checked his notes. "Thirty-seven days."

"And he's the kid that Tony replaced."

"Right," said Berger. "Sounded a little like Tony. Everything's fine and then one day he's all upset, he won't talk about it, and then he's gone." He looked across the desk at me. "Does that mean anything to you, hint at anything at all?"

"They both worked for Bigelow," I said. "Beyond that . . ."

"Word has it that he's fallen on hard times."

"The place is falling apart," I agreed. "But selling a three-million-dollar yearling that's never set foot on a track has to help."

"Maybe," he said.

"Maybe?" I repeated.

"You know these multi-millionaires," he said. "They can spend more in a day than you or I make in a decade."

"Actually," I said, "I don't know these multi-millionaires, at least not as well as I'd like to—but I'll take your word for it."

"Anyway," said Berger, "if I find that either kid has been harmed—or perhaps both of them—I figure maybe there's a connection."

"Let's hope they're both having fun in the sun, but, yeah," I agreed. "Is the guy who took the call around today?"

He looked at the notes again. "Drew MacDonald," he said. "Yeah, I think he's just starting the night shift, and I'm pretty sure he's on desk duty this week. Let me see." He picked up his phone, punched in three numbers, and waited a minute. "Drew? Lou Berger here. Can you stop by my office for a minute? Thanks."

He turned to me. "He's on his way."

A moment later the door opened, and a tall, slender man, graying at the sides and wearing thick glasses, entered the office.

"Drew, say hello to Eli Paxton. He's a detective from Cincinnati, here on a case."

"Public?" asked MacDonald, extending his hand.

"Private," I replied, taking and shaking it.

"So what can I do for you, Mr. Paxton?"

"Call me Eli," I said. "I'm looking for a young man who's disappeared, and the circumstances are very similar, at least on the surface, to one you dealt with last month."

"I don't know," he said dubiously. "Runaway kids are a dime a dozen these days."

"You'll remember this one, Drew," said Berger.

"Okay," answered MacDonald. "Who was it?"

"Billy Paulson."

MacDonald shook his head. "Unless your kid worked for Travis Bigelow and thought someone might kill him, you're barking up the wrong tree, Eli."

"My kid worked for Bigelow," I said.

Suddenly MacDonald looked interested. "And he thought his life was in danger?"

"I don't know," I answered. "But he was worried as all hell about something."

"About what?"

"Again, I don't know," I said. "But he told me one night that he was worried, he had to figure out what to do, and he might want my advice in the morning."

"And did he ask for it?"

I shook my head. "I never saw him again."

"Interesting," said MacDonald. "And they both worked for Bigelow?"

"Yes."

"Were they friends?"

"I don't think they knew each other. My kid was hired when yours vanished. They both wound up caring for the same horse."

"Grooms care for more than one horse," noted MacDonald.

"Not at sales time, and not when he's worth over three million dollars," put in Berger.

"They both handled that Trojan colt?" asked MacDonald.

"So I'm told. I know Tony—*my* kid—did."

"Tell you what," said MacDonald. "It's late for you and early for me. I have a few hours of paperwork to do, but when I finish I'll hunt up everything we have on Billy Paulson and our search for him. Let's meet for breakfast—well, your breakfast, my dinner—at eight tomorrow morning, and I'll turn it over to you, and we'll see if there's any unifying thread."

"Sounds good to me," I said. "Where do you want to meet?"

"Tilly's," he said. "It's a hash house just half a mile south of here. You can't miss it."

"I feel like a fifth wheel," said Berger. "Tell you what. I'll come in a bit early tomorrow, before you fill your faces—and Eli, stand clear of this man when he starts pouring ketchup—and I'll see if we have any other reports of missing persons, or anything else, connected with Bigelow or Mill Creek."

We all shook hands, MacDonald went back to his office, and I drove to the motel in a heavy rainstorm, where I spent an evening watching TV shows where the private eye and the cops hated each other and spent half of every episode trying to undermine each other's work.

10.

I put in a wake-up call for seven o'clock, shaved without cutting myself too many times (I never could stand electric razors), showered without letting too much water spill onto the floor, found I didn't have any clean shirts or socks left—I was supposed to be back in Cincinnati two days ago—and had the desk clerk point me to a laundry, where I dropped off some shirts, underwear, and socks on my way to meet Mac-Donald for breakfast.

Tilly's looked like a garage that had fallen on hard times. It had a couple of windows, and a couple of booths, and a bunch of stools at the breakfast counter, and it had Tilly herself, who was about fifty pounds overweight, all of it muscle. I looked around, didn't see MacDonald, though the place wasn't hurting for business, and sat down at a booth. There was a jukebox selection on the wall, and as I read through the selections I began to feel more and more at home. There was Sinatra, and Rosy Clooney, and Crosby, and Sarah Vaughan, and the Andrews Sisters, and no bands with idiotic names and electric instruments whose notion of music was screaming at the top of their lungs. I blew a quarter on Helen O'Connell and Bob Eberle singing "Tangerine" and ordered a cup of coffee, and just as the song ended, Drew MacDonald entered the place, peered through his thick glasses, spotted me, and walked over to sit opposite me.

"Good morning, Eli," he said. "I assume you had no trouble finding this place?"

"None," I said. "If Tilly's food is as good as her music, I may try to coax her into moving to Cincinnati."

"Not unless you want an even bigger war than the one over who owns the Ohio River where it runs between Kentucky and Ohio." He smiled. "Took 'em more than a century to resolve that one in court."

"Morning, Drew," yelled Tilly from behind the counter.

"The usual," he replied, then turned to me. "How about you?"

"I'll have the same."

"But you don't even know what it is."

"I know it hasn't killed you yet," I said.

"What the hell," he said with a shrug. "Hey, Tilly, make it two—one for me, one for my friend."

"So," I said, "what have you got for me?"

He sighed heavily. "Bits and pieces. I don't know if they fit or not, but you're welcome to them."

"Such as?"

"Let me see. Where to start?" he said, frowning. "Or rather, who to start with?"

"There's more than Billy Paulson?" I asked.

"I don't know," he said. "That's up to you to find out. But let's start with Paulson."

"Shoot."

"He phoned the station thirty-eight days ago. He didn't expressly ask for me, just for any cop, and my phone wasn't in use at the moment. He told me that he'd learned something, or discovered something, or found something out—he was a little vague, not purposely; I think he just wasn't a clear thinker, at least not that day—and that he was scared. I questioned him, but he didn't want to tell me what was frightening him, just that he wanted a name to ask for if he came to some decision or other and wanted to call back. He also wanted us to search for him every day if he didn't check in with us—and we did, for a few days anyway."

"Did he say what he might call back about?" I asked.

MacDonald shook his head. "Could have been to tell me what was frightening him, could even have been to ask for police protection. He was pretty vague. All I could get out of him was name, rank, and serial number . . . which is to say his name and where he worked, which doubled as his address. Mighty few grooms go home at night. One of the benefits of being a groom is that you don't pay room and board." He smiled. "It's a consideration at any level. My wife says when we retire—she's working at Walgreen's—we should buy a little farm, partly for some retirement income and mainly because the house comes with the farm."

"Okay," I said. "So the kid worked for Bigelow. And you never heard from him again."

"That's right."

"That's all you had last night."

He nodded. "That was everything I had last night. Today I've got a little more."

"Okay."

"I can supply the dots. I don't know if they can be connected, but that'll be your job."

"We'll see," I said. "What have you got?"

He was about to answer when Tilly approached the table and gave us each a plate of eggs Benedict smothered in hollandaise sauce, plus hash browns and toast, as well as a cup of coffee for MacDonald and a refill for me.

"Looks good," I remarked.

"Tastes even better," he said. "Trust me on this." He turned to Tilly. "Someday I'm going to kidnap you, cart you off to a desert island, and have you cook just for me."

"Get me a new stove and freezer and I just might go willingly," she said with a smile, and retreated to her workplace behind the counter.

"So," I said, "you were about to tell me something?"

"A few things. We figured that if the kid actually learned anything dangerous, he had to have learned it at Mill Creek Farm, since he lived there and according to his coworkers hadn't driven anywhere in his ancient Rambler for almost a week."

"Makes sense," I agreed.

"So we did a little research on Bigelow," he continued. "The man's in deep financial trouble."

"Well, until two days ago, anyway," I said. "His place is falling apart. And it's the kind of damage that looks like it's been that way and getting worse for a few years."

"It's more than the farm," said MacDonald. "He needed money to buy the damned farm in the first place. The clothing company he owned went belly-up ten years ago, and the brokerage house he had a share in closed its doors four years ago." He paused. "Not only that, but he owned three shares in Moonbeam and a share in Trojan, and he sold them all in the past eighteen months."

"What would they have been worth?"

"Whatever the market will bear," answered MacDonald. "Trojan syndicated into forty shares for thirty million dollars when he retired, so theoretically that makes each share worth about three-quarters of a million, but it's a free market, so if you want a share and no one will sell for that price, you pay a million or a million and a half or whatever it takes. And of course, if he produces ten or twelve stakes winners in his first crop, and maybe a champion or two, it'll be four or five times that much two years from now. Moonbeam is an established sire, maybe a dozen years old, so his price is pretty much set. Near as I can tell, shares are trading for about four hundred thousand.

"What do you get for a share?"

"Depending on the stallion and the agreement, one or two stud services a year. You can use them on your own mares or sell one or both to other mare owners."

"So he made maybe two million dollars in the last year or so just selling those shares, and he still needed money?"

"He did when Billy Paulson went missing," said MacDonald. "I don't know about now. He just got over three million for the Trojan colt, and he sold five others for another million and a quarter total." He paused. "That's all I've got on Bigelow. The man was in trouble before the sale. He just picked up a quick four mil, so that may have gotten him free and clear. As for the kid, maybe he stumbled on something, some phony business deal Bigelow was going to dupe investors with." He shrugged. "Or maybe not."

"Well, it's something to look into, if my clients want to pursue the case," I said.

"Dig in, Eli," he said. "I kid you not, this is the best eggs Benedict in the state."

I took a bite. Damned if he wasn't right.

"So," I said, wolfing down a couple more mouthfuls, "is that all you've got?"

"Probably," he answered. "I don't know."

"*What* don't you know?"

"If I've got anything else. It seems awfully tenuous. The only connection is the date."

"Try me."

"Okay," said MacDonald. "Another thing I did was check our files for anything unusual, anything of interest, the day Billy Paulson vanished." He looked across the table at me. "You ever hear of Horatio Jimenez?"

"Sounds like a nightclub comedian."

He shook his head. "Not hardly."

"Okay," I said. "Who is he?"

"A shooter from New Mexico."

"Mob?"

"Indy."

"So what's he got to do with Paulson or Bigelow?" I asked.

"Probably nothing," answered MacDonald. "I have no proof, not even a hint that Bigelow knows him or even knows who he is, or that they ever had any dealings, and I'll bet the farm we're going to buy that he didn't know Paulson."

"So why mention him at all?"

"Because someone answering his description—we think it was him, but we don't know for sure—was spotted in town the day Paulson vanished and hasn't been seen since. Until now."

"Now?" I repeated.

"He occasionally stops by during sales week. Never attends the sale itself, never spends more than an evening here. We figure he's just renewing contacts—I mean, hell, the guys who can afford him are precisely the guys who can blow big money on untried yearlings—and this time we got a positive identification. Anyway, I checked the Hilton Suites, which is where he usually stays when he's in town, and where we assume he stayed last month."

"So did he have a room there?"

MacDonald shrugged helplessly. "Who knows? Hitters don't travel under their own names, and they invariably pay cash for everything so they don't leave a trail. Anyway, he was out of there the next morning. Now, even if it was him, maybe he was just on his way to New York or Chicago—they like out-of-town shooters in the big cities—or maybe he actually had business here. And if he did, we don't know what it was, and there's no reason in the world to link it to Bigelow or Paulson."

"Anything else?"

He shook his head. "That's everything."

"No one else vanished from Bigelow's farm?" I persisted.

"As far as I can tell, no one else even quit. He must pay the staff on time. Most of them live hand to mouth; pay 'em late once or twice and they're gone. But outside of those two grooms, he hasn't lost anyone since Frank Standish started working for him maybe six months ago."

"I met him," I said. "Seems like a nice enough guy."

"He must be," agreed MacDonald. "Anyway, they seem to like working for him. Usually there's a pretty regular turnover, except when you get one of these billionaires who pays too much and wants everyone to feel like a big happy family."

"I get the feeling that was never Bigelow's problem," I said wryly.

"I don't know what his problems are, but he seems to have his share of them. Every now and then, when one of these huge operations goes down the drain, I can't help but ask myself: they had to be worth millions, probably tens of millions, to get into the game. Where the hell did it all go?"

"I'd say on horses who quit fifty yards short of six furlongs," I answered. "But that's not Bigelow's problem. He never ran his horses."

"Well, he probably bought some wrong horses," said MacDonald. "Or some wrong mares, actually. You can't be much of a market breeder without a top broodmare band, and since he didn't race, he had to buy them."

"I don't know much about breeding," I said. "My interest in racing is pretty much limited to buying two-dollar tickets and ripping them up a few minutes later…but I'd have to say that if he can sell one yearling for over three million, Trojan colt or not, and five more non-Trojans for over a million total, he must have an eye for a broodmare."

"Him, or Frank Standish," replied MacDonald. "Well, Standish's predecessor. It's too soon for any mare Standish told him to buy to have a foal ready for market. Besides, from what I can tell, he probably couldn't drop more than fifty grand or so on any mare this year."

"Fifty grand will buy you a hell of a nice car," I said.

"Yeah, but it won't buy you the kind of mare you want to breed to Trojan or Moonbeam."

"Okay, I'll take your word for it."

He yawned. "If that's everything, I'm off to grab forty or fifty winks. Let me know if you find out anything interesting. And breakfast is on the Lexington police department."

"Thanks," I said, sliding out of the booth and getting to my feet as he did the same opposite me.

"You think anything I told you will help with your missing kid?"

"I don't know," I admitted. "I think the first thing I'd better do is check in with his parents and see if they want to keep spending their money."

"And if they do?"

"Then I've still got to find out what he thought he knew and why he thought he might have to talk to me about it the next day."

He shook my hand. "Good luck, Eli."

"Thanks," I said. "I have a feeling I'll be needing it."

11.

The Sanders lived in a modest little ranch house on the edge of town—not the rich, thoroughbred-laden edge of town, the *other* edge. It was after nine-thirty when I pulled into their driveway and got out of the car. I figured Mr. Sanders would already have left for work, but they were both at home and had walked out to greet me before I was halfway to their door.

"Good morning, Mr. Paxton," said Sanders. "Do you have any news for us?"

I shook my head. "I'm afraid not," I said. "I just thought I'd give you an update on what I haven't found, and see if you want me to keep looking."

I could tell by the way their faces fell that despite what I'd told them when they hired me, they'd pretty much expected me to have found Tony by now. They escorted me into the living room where Mrs. Sanders offered me, in quick succession, coffee, wine, beer, and brandy, all of which I turned down.

"Let me begin by asking you a pair of strange questions," I said as they sat together on a couch and learned forward intently. "First, did Tony ever mention another Mill Creek groom, a young man named Billy Paulson?" I held up a hand before they could answer. "Now, this is going to sound strange, but he never met this Paulson fellow. They couldn't possibly have been friends. I just want to know if you ever heard him mention Paulson's name."

Sanders shook his head. "No, not to the best of my memory."

I turned to Mrs. Sanders. "And you, ma'am?"

"No, Mr. Paxton."

"All right," I said. "My other question: did Tony ever talk about Bigelow's finances?"

"He was just a kid working there," said Sanders. "He wouldn't know anything about that."

"He never talked about people dunning Bigelow for money?" I persisted. "Or about the sorry condition of the property? Or about maybe some paychecks bouncing?"

Sanders shook his head again. "He was only there a month, and he spent all his time with the horses. Well, with the one horse, anyway."

"He could have heard rumors or other people talking," I continued.

"If he did, he kept it to himself," said Mrs. Sanders.

"Okay," I said. "I only have one more question. Did he or any of his associates—friends, trainers, jockeys, anyone in the industry—ever mention a man named Horatio Jimenez?"

They looked at each other, each clearly hoping the name rang a bell with the other so they could give me something to go on, since all their other answers had been negative. But finally they both shook their heads. Neither had heard of him, which in my opinion was an exceptionally healthy state of affairs.

"Okay, that's all I needed to ask," I said.

"What does it mean?" replied Sanders. "You've clearly learned something about Tony."

"I'm hoping that I haven't," I said.

He stared at me questioningly. "I don't understand," he said at last.

"There are two possibilities," I explained. "One is that, for whatever reason, he's left town and could be anywhere in, or even out of, the country. The other is that he hasn't left town. That's the possibility I'm looking into first, since it saves you the expense of flying me all over the country."

"I see," he said.

"And if he's in town, there are two possibilities," I said. "Either he's alive or he's not."

There was a sharp intake of breath from Mrs. Sanders, but she continued staring right at me.

"I don't mean to upset you, ma'am," I continued. "But I'd be remiss if I didn't explain what I was doing and why."

"I understand," she said. "Please go on."

"No one's seen him since the night before the sale. His girlfriend—"

"He doesn't have one, not anymore," she interrupted.

"He's been seeing her regularly, ma'am," I said. "Anyway, she hasn't seen him since before the sale, hasn't heard from him. He mentioned nothing about leaving or any future plans." I paused while it sank in that Tony was still seeing Nanette. "If there was any foul play, or the promise of foul play such that Tony had to vanish without a word to anyone, it almost certainly originates in some way at Mill Creek Farm. He spent the last month living there, and from what I can understand Travis Bigelow is in serious financial trouble."

"Bigelow?" scoffed Sanders. "My god, he's a millionaire!"

"Well, a million doesn't go as far as it used to," I replied. "If there was a problem for Tony, it had to have originated at the farm. I haven't turned anything up so far. I may never. So I thought I should come over, fill you in, and ask you: do you want me to keep working on the case? At this point, I couldn't swear that he isn't sunning himself in Malibu, I can't swear that whatever was bothering him that last night was real or meaningful, and I can't even swear that he's alive. I'll keep looking as long as you want, but I warn you that it can get very expensive."

"Let's go at least a few more days," said Sanders. "If in a week you're no further along, maybe we'll have to reconsider. But damn it, he's our son, our only one!"

"Are you in agreement, Mrs. Sanders?" I asked, turning to her. "I can step outside if you want to discuss it."

She seemed about to say something, then straightened her back and stared into my eyes.

"Find my boy," she said.

12.

I took another look around Mill Creek, but I couldn't find anything that might have suggested what happened to either groom. Standish escorted me around; he seemed friendly enough, but I gathered visitors weren't allowed to go wandering on their own. Hard times for Bigelow or not, there was still some valuable horseflesh on the property.

"So, have you turned anything up yet?"

I shook my head. "Not really. Did Billy Paulson ever give you the idea that he was in trouble?"

"No. He seemed a happy, hardworking kid." He frowned. "But I thought you were supposed to be looking for Tony Sanders."

"I am. But when two kids vanish a month apart from the same place, in fact from the very same job, it makes sense to see if there's a connection. Did Paulson live here?"

"Just about all the younger grooms do," answered Standish. "But the cops took all his stuff. We've got someone else in his room now."

Just then a van pulled up, and Frank turned to me. "Excuse me," he said, "but I've got to welcome Big Mama back."

"Big Mama?" I repeated.

He smiled. "The mother of the Trojan colt. She was barren last year, and her first couple of breedings this year didn't take. If she missed this time, that's it for another year."

"You can't keep trying until she's pregnant?"

"We could," he answered as we walked toward the van. "But all racehorses have an arbitrary birthday of January 1, and a late June or early July foal would be at too much of a disadvantage. By the time he caught up physically with his rivals, all the good ones would be retired."

"So is this going to be another Trojan colt?" I asked.

He shook his head. "Mr. Bigelow sold his share of Trojan close to two years ago. This time Tyrone's mother went to Touchdown Pass."

"I never saw him," I said, "not even on TV."

"Happens a lot with West Coast horses, especially if they don't run in the Triple Crown or the Breeders' Cup."

"She's just flown back from California?" I asked.

He smiled. "No, from about fifteen miles down the road. They may run in California and New York and elsewhere, but ninety percent of the good ones retire to Kentucky."

The van had stopped, and the driver came around the back, slid out a ramp for the mare to walk down, and opened the door at the back. He then led her out by a rope attached to her halter.

"I'll take her from here, George," said Standish.

"Hope we got something this time, Harry," replied the driver. "Anyway, she looks happy."

"Probably happy just to be out of the van," said Standish. He began leading her to a pasture, and I walked alongside him.

"What would a foal be worth?" I asked.

He shrugged. "Who knows?" he said. "A lot depends on Tyrone. He wins the Champagne or the Futurity or one of the other major stakes for two-year-olds, this one would go for a couple of million, especially if it's a boy. He runs like a cheap claimer, and this one's price plummets."

"Even though it's not the same sire?"

"A lot of investors and writers forget it, but Momma supplies half the genes."

"Yeah," I said. "I suppose when Poppa produces a hundred foals a year and Momma produces one, it's easy to forget."

"Take a look at the percentages, if you want to see something interesting."

"I don't follow you."

"The most successful stallion in history, in terms of the percentage of stakes winners he sired, was Bold Ruler. You know what that percentage was?"

"I have no idea," I replied.

"Twenty-five percent," said Standish. "One-quarter of all his foals won stakes races. The average for the breed is something less than one percent. Are you impressed?"

"I'm impressed," I said.

"You know how many mares have produced more than twenty-five percent stakes winners?" he asked with a smile.

"No."

"Neither do I," he answered. "But it's well over two hundred." He patted the mare on the neck. "People forget that it takes more than a sire, but we remember, don't we, baby?"

The mare nickered at him, and a moment later he turned her loose in an empty pasture. She trotted once around it, as if to make sure it was the one she remembered, and then settled down to do some serious grazing.

"Anything else I can answer or help you with before I make my rounds?" asked Standish.

"Just one thing," I said. "You ever hear of a man named Horatio—" I stopped in mid-sentence as a thought hit me. "Oh, shit!"

"Horatio Oh Shit?" he replied with a grin.

"Sorry," I said. "I just thought of something. Have you got a phone in one of these barns?"

"Yeah, but they're just connected to my office. You can't dial out."

"Okay," I said. "I'll just drive down the road until I come to a pay phone."

"They're getting rare as hen's teeth," said Standish. "Why don't you just use your cell phone?"

"Battery's dead," I said, which was easier—and quicker—than explaining why I don't like or trust cell phones. It's not just that they're newfangled, it's not just that there should be times when no one can bother you, it's not even that being a phone seems to be the least of their functions these days. But if you've got your checking and savings account numbers and all your passwords and e-mail addresses and the like on your cell phone, any pickpocket can steal your entire life from you. Not that I had anything worth stealing except Marlowe, and anyone who wanted him was welcome to him, but I still objected to the damned things on principle.

I walked quickly to my car, and when the first three gas stations I passed didn't have pay phones, I just drove on to the police station, figuring that it was another few minutes in the car versus maybe two hours trying to find a phone.

I pulled up, got out, blew a kiss to Bernice as I walked past, and let myself into MacDonald's office. It was empty, of course; we'd had breakfast just a few hours ago, but while that was the start of my day, it was the end of his.

I turned around, left the office, and went to Lou Berger's office instead.

"Hi, Eli," he said. "You look . . . I don't know—tense or excited, or perhaps you've been overcome with lust for Bernice. What can I do for you?"

"I need to know something," I said. "MacDonald probably has it at his fingertips, but he's asleep."

"What is it?" he said. "If the answer's in the office, I can find it without too much trouble."

"You guys told me that Horatio Jimenez was here the day Tyrone was sold. What time was he spotted?"

"Give me a minute," he said, getting to his feet. "I know where Drew files his current cases."

"Is it his case?"

"Ever since you spoke to him," confirmed Berger. "I don't know who else's it could be. I'll be right back."

He walked down the hall to MacDonald's office and returned about two minutes later.

"Our first report of Jimenez being in town came at six in the evening, when he was spotted checking into the Hilton Suites. We kept an eye out for him at the pavilion, but he never showed."

"Okay," I said. "I knew I was missing something."

"What?"

"There can't be a connection."

"What kind of connection?" said Berger. "I'm not following you."

"Since Jimenez is a hitter and he came to Lexington the day Tony vanished, it was easy to think he might have had something to do with it. But he couldn't have."

"Just out of curiosity, why not?"

"Because he didn't have time to get to the barn before I got back from dinner, and by then Tony was already worried about . . . well, about whatever it was that had him so upset."

"Couldn't he have stopped by on his way to the hotel?" asked Berger.

I shook my head. "I was there all day. I didn't go out for dinner 'til about six, and there's no way he could have talked to Tony after I left and still checked in around six. And I was back by a quarter to seven."

"Okay," said Berger. "I know it's no help to you, but you just made the Lexington police force's job a little easier. It's comforting to know we don't have to try to extradite a well-known shooter who might have friends in this town. I hope to hell the kid is having the time of his life on some beach."

"I just hope he checks in so we know he's okay."

"If he does, you're out of a job," said Berger with a smile.

"Beats the hell out of sitting next to his parents at the funeral," I replied.

"True enough," he agreed. He checked his watch. "I hate to throw you out, Eli, but I've got a ton of paperwork to do."

"Not a problem," I said. "Time for me to get back to work too. I just wanted to make sure about Jimenez. At least he's out of the picture."

"Out of your picture," Berger corrected me.

"Oh?"

He smiled wryly. "The fact that he didn't see the Sanders kid while you were having dinner is all well and good, and I'm happy for you and the kid's parents—but I still have to find out what a hired killer was doing in Lexington during the yearling sales."

13.

Fishbein's wasn't doing much business when I pulled up. There was an old gent with a cane and an oxygen bottle arguing with the pharmacist about something, and a boy who wouldn't be shaving for another four years trying to convince the cashier he really was old enough to buy a pack of Marlboros.

Nan was restocking some shelves, but she stopped the second she saw me approaching.

"Have you found him?" she asked eagerly.

I shook my head. "No, I'm still looking."

"I told you everything I know the last time you were here," she said.

"I know."

"Then why are you back?" she asked. "Why aren't you out looking for him?"

"Where do you think I should look?" I replied.

"How do I know?" she said. "You're the cop."

"The detective," I corrected her.

She shrugged. "Whatever."

"Anyway, I need to know more about Tony—what he liked, what he ate, where he went to relax, anything at all you can tell me."

"He liked hamburgers," answered Nan. "Oh, and pizza. Always the same: it had to have sausage and mushrooms and nothing else, or he wouldn't eat it."

"Did he drink?"

"You mean, like alcohol?"

"Yes," I said.

"Once in a while a beer, never anything more than that. Even before he got the Trojan colt he always had expensive horses in his care

82

at his other jobs, and he never wanted to screw up—pardon my language—by forgetting to feed them or do whatever he was supposed to do because he was drunk."

"Sounds like the young man I met," I said. "Is there anything else you can tell me—anything at all? Did he bowl? Go to the movies much? Anything you can remember?"

She shook her head. "He was devoted to whatever horse that was in his care. I mean, hell, if the horse coughed once or took one bad step, he'd call to tell me he wouldn't be picking me up after work and I'd have to take the bus home."

"Shit!" I muttered.

"I beg your pardon?"

"I'm an idiot!" I said. "He drove you home?"

"Yes. Or to dinner."

"In his own car?"

"Who else's?" she replied with a frown.

"I mean that," I persisted. "It was his car, not his parents'?"

"Yes."

"Do you know what kind it was?"

"A light-blue Plymouth, from 1997 or 1998, I think. Very old, anyway."

"Two doors or four?"

"Two. And with lots of rust on it. Why?"

"It's another lead," I said. "If I can find his car, maybe he'll be with it."

"He bought it about a year ago, when his last one died," she replied. "It was even older."

"You wouldn't know the license number?"

She shook her head. "He said if Tyrone set a sales record, he was going to get a vanity plate with Tyrone's name on it."

"Okay," I said. "Thank you, Nan."

"I hope whatever I said was useful."

"You and me both," I told her.

I went out to the car and drove back to the police station.

"We're going to start charging you rent," said Bernice with a smile as I walked in.

"If you'll loan it to me," I said, returning her smile. "Either of my boys in?"

"Lou's still here for another half hour or so," she replied. "Drew's not due in for another hour, but he's usually fifteen or twenty minutes early."

"Thanks," I said, walking to Berger's office.

He looked up from a pile of papers. "One of us looks happy," he said. "What have you got?"

"Nothing yet," I said. "If I told you that Tony Sanders owned a beat-up octogenarian Plymouth, could you hunt up the license plate?"

"Sure," he said, turning to his computer and tapping in a sentence or two. Then he turned back to me. "The license bureau should have something back to me in a couple of minutes. Maybe a little longer, since I don't know his legal address."

"Thanks," I said. "Nan—his girlfriend—thinks it's a Plymouth, but she didn't know the model and wasn't sure about the year."

"No problem," responded Berger. "If it's carrying a Kentucky plate, we'll have all the information when they send me the number."

"Good," I said. "If I didn't know better, I'd say the kid was hiding—and doing a damned good job of it."

"Why would he hide?"

"Why would he disappear? He loved his work and he had a good-looking girlfriend."

"Maybe he was unhappy because he was about to lose the Trojan colt."

I shook my head. "He loves the horses, but I don't think he loved the horse, if you see what I mean."

"I see it," replied Berger. "The question is: Did he see it?"

"I spent a couple of days with him," I said. "He struck me as a young man who had his head screwed on right."

His computer beeped, and he turned to look at the screen, where a message was coming in. He stared at it, frowned, and reached for his phone. He punched out three numbers, which implied that it was an inter-department call, waited for a minute, then said: "Hello. This is Lou Berger . . . yeah, I got your message. I just wanted to call to confirm it. Will you read it aloud to me?" He waited a moment, still frowning, then said, "Thanks," and hung up the phone.

"What is it?" I asked.

"We had some rain last night," he began. "Did it hit you before you got to your motel?"

"Yeah, I drove back through it," I said.

"It rained two or three more times during the night."

"Okay, it rained," I said. "What does that have to do with the license plate?"

"We found it and the car," Berger said. "A 1998 Plymouth Prowler."

He was still frowning.

"What else?" I said.

"It was parked at a Kroger supermarket over near Leestown Road. Been there for a couple of days. No one minded. Happens all the time at stores with big parking lots, like Kroger and Walmart. Guy's taking a plane trip and doesn't want to pay airport parking, so he parks there and has a friend drop him at the terminal. They probably wouldn't have reported it for another week, but they were worried because the top was down and it was getting rained on."

"Where's Leestown Road?" I asked.

He shook his head sadly. "Not near any friend he's got, not near the blonde's apartment, not near any farm he's ever worked at."

"Well, he sure as hell didn't take a plane anywhere," I said. "Kid didn't have two cents to rub together."

"Could he have borrowed it?"

"From a couple of friends who haven't seen him in over a week, or a girl who's worried sick about him and has no idea where he is?" I replied. "I doubt it like all hell."

"So he probably didn't run away, and he hasn't thought to pick up his car," said Berger, and I could see that he was thinking the same thing I was.

"Okay," I said. "I need answers to two questions. The first is what the hell he was doing at or near that Kroger. There have to be closer ones if all he wanted was to buy some food."

"And the second?"

"Who wanted him dead and why?"

"You think?" he asked.

"Yeah," I said. "I think. And you?"

"Makes sense." He leaned back on his chair and clasped his hands behind his head. "We'll help you any way we can, Eli, and of course we'll kept this quiet until we officially know for a fact that he's dead." He grimaced. "But it feels right."

I sighed heavily. "Yeah, it does."

"Well, I guess we're about to find out how good a detective you are," he said. "You've eliminated Horatio Jimenez. That leaves just three hundred thousand suspects and a body—if there's a body."

"Damn," I said. "I had to be a detective. Hell, I could be pitching for the Reds right now."

"You were a ballplayer?" he asked.

"No."

He frowned. "Then I don't understand."

I flashed him a totally humorless smile. "How much harder could it be than this?"

14.

They towed the car into their garage in less than an hour, and I stopped by to look it over. Not that I expected to find anything useful.

It was a 1998 Prowler, pretty beat up. The left front bumper had been caved in by another car, not enough to affect the wheel, but fixing it would have cost more than the car was worth on the market. Air-conditioning wasn't working. Tony (or a previous owner) had torn the seat belts out and knew enough about cars so that there were no annoying flashing lights or beeping sounds because the belts weren't fastened. There was a CD player and a ton of the junk that passes for music these days. And the car had logged 262,407 miles and was still running.

The top was down, which is the only way it would have been reported in less than a week or two. I checked the mechanism, and it was working. I remembered back to the night he vanished. It was clearly going to rain, probably had already sprinkled some, which meant Tony didn't figure to be wherever he was for long or he'd have put the top up.

My next stop was Mill Creek, where I had Standish get one of Bigelow's house flunkies to print out the addresses of everyone who'd worked for him for the past half year. I didn't know my way around Lexington very well, so I headed back to the station, showed the list to MacDonald, who'd shown up while I was gone, and asked him to put a mark next to anyone who lived within a few blocks of the Kroger lot, on the assumption that since he had a car, Tony wouldn't have walked more than two or three blocks from where he left it.

"Are you sure this is the entire list?" asked MacDonald after he'd studied it.

"I'm sure it's the entire list that they gave me," I replied. "I can't swear that it's complete or accurate, but I assume it is, because it'd be so easy to prove he left something off."

He handed the paper back to me. "I hate to tell you this, Eli, but not a single address on this list is within walking distance of the Kroger where he left the car."

I frowned. "Are you sure?"

He nodded. "I'm not a stranger to Lexington."

"It doesn't make any sense," I muttered. "The kid was worried. He told his girl, he told me. I've got a feeling he's dead. He was some-where between worried and scared the night he vanished. Why the hell did he drive to that particular lot, when none of his friends lived near there, Standish and Bigelow live on the farm, his parents are on the other side of town, so who the hell's left?"

"I ran a check on him last night," offered MacDonald. "No arrests, one speeding ticket a year ago, as far as we know he never ran with a gang."

"Why there?" I persisted. "If he thought his life was in danger, and he couldn't confide in anyone, he had a car—so why didn't he just take off and put five hundred miles between himself and Lexington by sunrise?" I paused, trying to come up with an answer. "I don't suppose there's a bus station anywhere near there?"

MacDonald shook his head. "Sorry, but no."

"Maybe I'd better drive over there and take a look for myself," I said.

"What are you looking for?"

I sighed. "Damned if I know," I admitted. "But that's where he thought to run or hide, so that's where I should at least look around." Then I got an idea. "Before I go, can you do me a favor?"

"Sure," said MacDonald. "What is it?"

"Find out if Tony had a credit card."

"Give me half a minute," he said. He activated his computer, and soon his fingers were flying over the keys. I envied him. I could barely type my name back in high school, I didn't get any better when I was with the Chicago police force, and I finally decided that computers and I were, if not mortal enemies, then at least destined never to be friends or partners.

"Okay," he said, looking up.

"Okay what?" I asked.

"Tony didn't have a credit card."

"Shit!" I said. "Then there's no way to find out if he bought anything at Kroger's."

"They're a supermarket, Eli," he said with a smile. "They don't sell bullets."

"If he bought some food and didn't take it out to his car, he was clearly walking it to wherever he went next," I said. "It would mean he did know someone within walking distance."

MacDonald nodded his head. "You got a point," he agreed. "You don't bring food to guys who are threatening your life."

"I might as well get started."

"It's evening."

"A lot of the Cincinnati Krogers are open around the clock," I said. "Maybe this one is, too. Besides, it's still a few hours before midnight, even if it closes."

He shook his head. "You're not going to learn anything at the Kroger," he said. "But if you wander around the neighborhood in the dark, it won't be long before someone reports you to the police."

"They didn't report Tony," I said, and then realized there was a difference. "Of course, he knew where he was going, or at least I have to assume he did." I got to my feet. "Thanks for your help, Drew."

"Get something definite and we'll do more than help," he promised.

"I'll count on that," I said. "I'm just a detective. Being a hero is another union."

We shook hands, and I began walking to the exit.

"Don't you ever sleep?" asked Bernice with a smile.

"Don't you?" I replied, returning the smile.

"I'm getting time and a half until they hire more help," she said. "How about you?"

"I'm not getting shot at. I consider that even better than time and a half."

She laughed, and then I was out the door and into the Ford. I started it, turned the Reds-Pirates game on the radio, pulled a Lexington street map out of my glove compartment, and studied it for a minute. I knew that Bill Striker insisted that his entire staff have GPSs in their cars, but the few times I'd been in a car with one, I found it intrusive as all hell, like your mother-in-law looking over your shoulder and telling you to turn here and stop there.

I began driving, accidently ran a red light when the Pirates' center fielder made a circus catch and robbed Joey Votto of a bases-clearing double, but in a few minutes I was at the Leestown Road Kroger. I pulled into the lot, got out of the car, looked around (though I had no idea what I was looking for), and finally entered the store.

It looked like any other Kroger—huge and efficient. I saw an Hispanic stock boy—well, his hair was gray, but I've never been able to think of the guy who puts Cheerios and Special K on the shelves as a stock man—and I walked over to him.

"I'm looking for something," I said.

"I'll be happy to help you, sir," he replied.

"Good," I said. "Where's the nearest horse farm?"

He looked puzzled for a minute. "This is a joke, right, sir?" he said at last.

"No," I answered. "Let me word it differently. Is there a horse farm within half a mile of here?"

He just shook his head and stared at me as if I might start taking off my clothes any second.

"You're sure?" I said.

"I'm sure."

"Okay, thanks," I said, walking to the exit before he could sound some hidden alarm.

I walked directly to my car, found out that Brandon Phillips had tied the score with a shot into the left field bleachers, and started driving.

It was a nice neighborhood, not as upscale as some, but nicer than anything I'd ever lived in. I began crisscrossing it for half a mile in each direction, first north-south, then east-west. Then I drove in a square around it.

"Damn it!" I muttered. "You were scared. You probably knew your life was in danger. You don't have any friends on any of the streets I just drove down. You couldn't talk to me. You couldn't talk to Nan. You couldn't talk to your parents. You felt you had to leave a three-million-dollar yearling behind, just to drive here, and . . . and what? Who did you see when you knew you were in trouble, and why don't we have any record of him?"

I drove around another half hour, looking at every house, every store, every outbuilding, and when I finally turned the car around and headed back to the Motel 6, I still didn't know.

15.

I dragged myself out of bed, drove by the laundry to pick up my shirts, socks, and underwear, went back to the motel long enough to shave, shower, and change, and then stopped by the police station, where MacDonald was just putting his desk in order prior to going home.

"You should have been here four or five hours ago, Eli," he said. "Lots of excitement."

"Oh?"

He nodded. "Two drunks we pulled in tried to kill each other." He smiled. "They were so far gone that we just let 'em swing. I don't think either of them came within eighteen inches of connecting with the other, but it wore them out enough that they became tractable enough to lock 'em away in separate cells so they can sleep it off."

"You want to see some real action," I replied, "come to a tailgate party at Paul Brown Stadium when the Bengals are playing."

"Certainly more action there than on the field, from what I read," he replied. Then: "So are you just stopping by to invite me to breakfast, or is there something I can do for you?"

"I went over to Leestown Road last night," I said.

"And didn't turn up a thing?" he asked.

"Right."

"I hate to say I told you so."

"There's a connection there somewhere," I said. "He had to have a reason to go there." I sighed. "I just haven't been able to find it."

"And you think you'll find it here?"

I shook my head. "No."

"Then what do you think we can do for you?"

"I'm just looking for connections," I said. "Any connection."

He frowned. "I don't follow you, Eli."

"I want to see your file on Billy Paulson."

"The groom Tony Sanders replaced?"

"Yeah."

"Do you have any reason to think something happened to Paulson?"

"No," I said. "Not yet."

"But you're hoping you might find a reason?"

I sighed. "I'm just hoping to find any kind of connection at all, besides the fact that they worked for Mill Creek and were in charge of the same horse."

"What the hell," he said. "I'll have my computer give you a printout on everything we've got on him, and while it's doing that I'll walk you over to the Evidence Room."

I frowned. "Evidence Room?" I repeated. "Then you think there was a crime."

"No. But nobody's stepped forward to claim the stuff we pulled out of his room at Mill Creek, and we had to stash it somewhere. Besides, this isn't Chicago or Manhattan," he added with a smile. "We don't have that many crimes, so we don't have that much evidence lying around."

"Lead the way," I said.

"Okay," he replied, getting to his feet and leading me down a corridor. "But if I help you find the kid, I want ten percent of your fee."

"No one's paying me a cent to find Billy Paulson," I replied. "That being the case, I will happily give you fifteen percent of nothing."

"And a breakfast."

"Okay," I agreed. "The best breakfast Tilly makes, as long as it's under five dollars."

He chuckled. "Welcome to 1972," he said. "They tell me there's a really good-looking two-year-old out there called Secretariat."

He stopped at a door, pulled a card out of his pocket, inserted it, and the door slid open silently, revealing a room that seemed composed almost entirely of metal shelves. It took MacDonald a couple of minutes to find what he was looking for, but finally he uttered a grunt of satisfaction, pulled down a cardboard box with "Billy Paulson" written on it with a Magic Marker, and handed it to me.

"The light's pretty poor here," I said. "You mind if I look at it in your office?"

"Tell you what," he said. "Jack Greenwald is on vacation. Give me a minute to clear it, and you can have his office for the next eight days, if you give me your word you won't open any drawers or file cabinets. They're all locked anyway."

"You got it."

"I'll have his computer activated too. You don't know his password, so you won't be able to access his files."

I shook my head. "Don't bother."

"You're sure?"

"I'm sure."

He shrugged. "Okay. Give me a couple of minutes."

He left the Evidence Room and was back in about five minutes.

"No problem," he announced. "We called Jim Simmons again, and he hasn't decided to hate you since we spoke to him two days ago. Also, my boss had heard about that thing you pulled off a while back, the one that started with a show dog and ended somewhere in Mexico."

Actually, it had ended in Cincinnati, but I wasn't allowed to say so, so I just smiled, thanked him, and followed him to Jack Greenwald's office, which was a carbon copy of Berger's and MacDonald's offices.

"The door will lock behind you, so you can just leave the box on the desk when you're done. Any time you want to access it again, just ask Bernice for a key card; I'll make sure she's got one for you."

"Will do," I said. "And thanks again, Drew."

"Television and the movies to the contrary, we're on the same side," he replied as he left the office and closed the door behind him.

I put the box on the desk, then sat down on Greenwald's swivel chair and removed the box's top. There wasn't much there, but I began going through it piece by piece, not knowing what I was looking for, just hoping something might trigger an idea.

Right on top of the little pile were a couple of paperback porn books, which at least meant he was healthy and he could read. There was a copy of Sports Illustrated, which meant that unlike Tony he at least had a passing interest in sports other than horse racing. There was a birthday card from what I assumed were his parents, or maybe an aunt and uncle: Robert and Wilma Paulson. Whoever they were, they lived in Connecticut. Another card—unsigned—from Mill Creek Farm and a third one from someone named Hal Chessman. It seemed bigger than the others, so I pulled it all the way out of the envelope and looked at it. It was a picture of a pudgy, balding guy holding a horse by the halter, and inscribed on it was "Take good care of my Derby winner" along with Chessman's signature. I made a mental note to find out who this Chessman was.

There were a couple of paid receipts, one for a pair of boots, one for some T-shirts. I assumed he was keeping them for tax purposes. There was a jockey's whip, pretty beat up. I'd always heard that they were called "popper" whips because they made a loud popping noise that startled a horse but didn't hurt him or leave any welts. Just for the hell of it I picked it up and slapped it down on my leg. It made a noise, all right—but it hurt like hell, and when I pulled up my trouser leg to look at my calf, I could see the welt already forming. So much for that particular myth. I probably outweigh the average jockey by seventy or eighty pounds, but every last one of them's got to be in better shape than me, so size and strength were a wash. Bottom line: the damned thing hurt.

Next was a little box containing some gold chains. The gold was already flaking off, so it was obvious they were cheap imitations, but then, if he was a kid who read porn, probably the young ladies he went after were cheap imitations too.

Then there was his shaving kit, which contained a long razor like they used in barber shops when I was a kid, which looked impressive but made it damned easy to slit your throat if you sneezed at the wrong moment. It also contained a toothbrush and toothpaste, and two spray bottles of a cheap men's cologne.

And, finally, there was the Little Black Book. I thumbed through it. Our Billy didn't have much of a social life. There were only five girls' names, plus one of those joints that will give you an advance on your paycheck for a mere twenty-five percent per week or whatever. I checked to see if any of the girls lived on Leestown Road. None did, and even if one of them had I wouldn't have known what to do about it anyway, since Leestown was where Tony had made his way, not Billy.

I closed the box. It hadn't told me much. The kid was old enough to shave, big enough to lust for women, he had a birthday sometime before he vanished, he had at least a passing interest in sports, and he either knew a jockey and kept the whip as a souvenir, or he was into really kinky sex.

End result: nothing.

In fact, there was only one loose end at all: Hal Chessman. And I was sure someone at Mill Creek could tell me who he was, and then the last possible link between Tony and Billy Paulson would be gone. I figured I'd spend another couple of days and then give the Sanders another chance to call it off just about the time I ran through every last possibility, no matter how obscure or unlikely, of finding their son.

16.

I realized that I hadn't eaten yet, so on the way out of the station I stopped by Bernice's desk and asked if she'd like to join me.

"Eli," she said, "you're either two hours late for breakfast or two hours early for lunch."

"You choose," I said. "I'll pop for either."

She smiled. "Some of us aren't self-employed, Eli. Some of us are salaried and have certain hours and obligations."

"Okay," I said with a sigh. "Sorry."

"On the other hand," she continued, "if you'd like to have dinner together, Dutch treat, the girl I've been subbing for came back from sick leave, and I'm off tonight at five."

"It's a date," I said.

"No," she replied. "It's a dinner. We'll play it by ear and see if it becomes a date."

Two guys entered the station just then and walked up to her with complaints, so I just nodded and waved good-bye as I headed out to the parking lot.

The only loose end—and even that was putting it too strong; the only name I didn't know in the Paulson disappearance—was Hal Chessman. I'd written down his return address, but rather than approach him cold I decided to learn what I could about him, so I drove out to Mill Creek, parked the car, and was headed off to the biggest of the barns when I spotted Frank Standish standing by a fence, watching five mares and their foals cantering around the paddock.

"Got a minute?" I asked as I walked up to him.

"Hi, Eli," he said. "We're going to have to start charging you board."

"I won't be here long enough today," I said. "I just need to ask you a question."

"You could have called on your cell phone," said Standish.

"I don't have your number," I said, which was true, even if it wasn't the reason.

"What do you think of the gray foal there?" he asked, and I looked at a baby gray horse cavorting next to its bay mother.

"Pretty," I said.

"Eli, they're all pretty. You think he'll make an imposing yearling?"

"How the hell would I know?"

"I think he's going to bring the biggest price of this batch," he said. "He's by Moon Base. Remember him?"

I shook my head. "Can't say that I do."

"He was quite a two-year-old," said Standish. "World of early speed. But when the races got longer . . ."

"They caught him?"

He nodded. "Tripped on his pedigree every time. But Momma's got some stamina in her pedigree." He turned to me. "Okay, you didn't come out to evaluate foals and guess what they'll sell for next year. How can I help you?"

"You ever hear of a guy named Hal Chessman?"

He chuckled. "Of course! He's the man I replaced here. In fact, he recommended me for the job."

"Can you tell me anything about him?" I asked.

"Sure. A real sweet guy, knows the business inside out. Never spent much time at the track, but he was supposed to be one of the best stallion managers around. Came here a few years ago when Bigelow thought he was going to import a couple of top stallions from Europe and maybe stand a few local ones as well, and when it didn't come to pass, he took a job at Bill Redcastle's farm managing Pit Boss, Marauder, three or four others."

"Where is Redcastle's place?"

"Maybe seven or eight miles west of here."

"And he left Mill Creek when?" I asked.

"Just about Christmas. I started the day after New Year's."

"He's still in town if I want to talk to him?"

"As far as I know. Hell, I got a birthday card from him a couple of months ago." He frowned. "I never thought to check the return address."

"Doesn't matter," I said. "I probably haven't got a damned thing to ask him."

"I've got one to ask you," said Standish.

"Shoot," I told him.

"Hal left here at the end of December. Tony Sanders didn't come to work for us until five or six weeks ago. What's one got to do with the other?"

"Not a thing, as far as I can tell," I answered.

"Then why—?"

"There are two missing grooms," I said. "I'm looking for connections."

He shook his head. "Eli, they didn't even know each other. I didn't hire Tony until Billy Paulson went missing." He paused. "You were referring to Billy, weren't you?"

I nodded. "Yes. I assume he was on good terms with Chessman?"

"Hell, everyone was on good terms with Hal. Sweetest guy you'd ever want to meet. Never abused a horse or a hired hand. And—this is in confidence, now—once or twice when Bigelow couldn't make the payroll, or was a few days late with it, Hal paid the grooms and exercise riders out of his own pocket."

"Sounds like he qualifies for sainthood."

"He's as close as you'll get to a saint in this business," agreed Standish. "Hell, when he left, most of the staff went with him. There were guys working two and three shifts when I got here, and even then the place was a mess until I could hire more help." He paused and looked at me. "What made you curious about him?"

"I was going through Billy Paulson's effects down at the local police station," I said. "The only thing I couldn't account for was a card—Christmas, I guess—that Chessman sent him. It was a name I didn't know, and I'm just tying up loose ends."

"Did you see the stick too?"

"The stick?" I repeated.

"Slang," he apologized. "The whip."

"Yeah," I said, and suddenly my calf started to smart.

"You know who once owned that?" asked Standish. "Eddie Arcaro, maybe the greatest jock of them all."

"Didn't he die twelve or fifteen years ago?" I asked.

He nodded. "Yes."

"So he couldn't have given Billy the whip."

"No, he gave it to the first farm Billy worked at. A two-year-old filly—a well-bred one—got loose and headed off toward the highway, and Billy caught up with her just before she ran into a truck. Sprained his ankle badly enough that they took him to the hospital—and to thank him, the owner gave him the whip. He carried it everywhere with him." Standish smiled at the memory. "I think it was his proudest possession, the stick Eddie Arcaro might have used on Citation or Kelso or Whirlaway. Billy never touched a horse with it, but he carried it everywhere."

"Thanks," I said.

"Are you okay?" he asked. "You look a little . . . I don't know . . . strange."

"Something I ate," I said. "I should stick to getting my breakfasts at Tilly's."

He nodded. "They say she's the best."

I made my way back to the car and began driving back to the motel. I had a feeling my expression hadn't changed. It had taken a minute to hit home, but when it finally did, the meaning of what I'd heard finally got through to me: the whip was Billy Paulson's most treasured possession. He was never without it.

But he was without it now.

And deep down in my gut I knew he was dead.

I'd started out looking for one missing kid. Suddenly I was sure I was dealing with two dead ones, and the only link between them was a horse that was probably a thousand miles away by now.

17.

I found a Walgreen's with a pay phone and decided to look up Hal Chessman's number, muttering a silent prayer that he *had* a listed number instead of a cell phone. The God of Detectives must have been listening, because sure enough, there he was in the phone book. He picked it up on the third ring. I told him who I was, that he could check me out with Frank Standish, and that I just needed a couple of minutes of his time. He agreed, told me how to get to his farm, and I told him I'd be there in twenty minutes.

Actually, it took half an hour. Nobody posts addresses out in horse farm country, and I hadn't asked the name of the farm he was working for. The first farm I stopped at couldn't help me, but the second told me how to get to Blue Banner, which was the farm that employed Chessman.

It was an impressive layout—white split-rail fences everywhere (with a discreetly hidden electric wire so none of the horses thought of jumping over it to see if the grass was greener in the next pasture). There was a huge stallion barn, with each stall leading out to its own paddock—which made sense; put two working stallions together and only one survives. There were other barns, all of them, like the fence, in beautiful condition. There was even a half-mile training track circling the place.

I pulled up to the main barn—I knew by now that trainers didn't live in the white-pillared mansions that seemed to accompany each farm—and approached the stallion barn. A young black man saw me, signaled for me to wait, then raced inside the barn. A moment later Chessman stepped out, pudgy and balding, just the way he looked on the card he'd sent to Billy Paulson.

"Mr. Paxton?" he said, extending his hand.

"Call me Eli," I replied.

"Fine," he said. "And I'm Hal. Come on into my office."

He turned and led me into the barn.

"That's Marauder," he said, pointing to a small bay stallion. "And down at the end of the row is Pit Boss. I could tell you who the other eight are, but those are the two everyone wants to see."

"I remember Pit Boss," I said. "Damned good horse."

He nodded. "Until he ran into Trojan. His first crop makes it to the sales ring next year. I hope they do half as well as Trojan's." He shook his head in wonderment. "That damned horse not only sired the sales topper, but his fillies averaged just about a million apiece. He's got a couple of colts coming up in the Saratoga sale in August. I'll be curious to see what they do. Hopefully the market's coming back before the Pit Bosses go up for sale." He stopped. "But you didn't come here to talk about that." He gestured to an open door. "Please, grab a seat. Care for some coffee?"

I walked through the doorway into what was probably once a pair of back-to-back tack rooms but had been converted into a very comfortable office with a desk, a phone, a computer, and some comfortable but not overstuffed leather furniture.

"Coffee would be fine," I said, taking a seat.

"With or without white stuff?"

"With."

He did something with his computer that was as incomprehensible to me as most things people do with them.

"Coming right up," he said, seating himself behind the desk. "So you're a private detective?"

"That's right."

"I'm not aware that I've ever met one. You don't look much like Humphrey Bogart. I think you're more the Robert Mitchum type."

"An old, tired Bob Mitchum, who wishes private eyes still wore battered fedoras so I could hide my bald spot," I said.

He laughed. "Damn! I like you already! I hope you're not here to arrest one of my young people."

I shook my head. "I just want a little information."

"If it's mine to give . . ."

A young man, just starting to grow a very sparse mustache, entered just then carrying a pair of cups on a tray.

"Our visitor gets this one," said Chessman, pointing to the one that had cream and, theoretically, sugar.

The young man carried the tray to me, I took the cup he indicated, and then he placed the tray and the remaining cup on the desk in front of Chessman.

"Thank you, Diablo," said Chessman. "Check on that mare that just arrived from California and make sure she's comfortable, that she's got enough water."

"Yessir, Mr. Chessman," he said, leaving.

I turned to Chessman. "Diablo?" I said.

"His real name's Bruce. What can it hurt to call him what he wants to be called?"

I decided I liked Chessman already, too.

"So who stole the Falcon?" he continued.

"Sydney Greenstreet and Peter Lorre, last I heard," I replied.

"What I meant was, who are you after?"

"I'm trying to find a kid you probably never heard of," I said. "Does the name Tony Sanders mean anything to you?"

He thought for a moment, then shook his head. "Why did you think it would?"

"I didn't."

He looked puzzled. "But—?"

"You asked, I answered. That's who I've been hired to find. It's not why I'm here. I wanted to ask a couple of questions about Billy Paulson."

"Nice kid," he said. "Always on time, never made excuses when he screwed up (which wasn't often), good with the horses, respectful of people. Never had a moment's trouble with him."

"I gather most of your staff followed you here from Bigelow's," I said. "Why didn't he?"

"He was supposed to," answered Chessman. "I promised each of them that they'd have a job here if they ever wanted it, and all but maybe three came away with me the day I moved over here. I knew Frank Standish would want his own crew, so taking mine didn't bother me, but I also knew Frank wouldn't get there until just after the first, so I told Billy and maybe six or seven others to stick around until Frank could replace them, that they still had jobs here whenever they showed up."

"And they all showed up shortly after Frank arrived at Mill Creek?"

He shook his head. "Two of them went elsewhere. Billy was supposed to come, but then he got the Trojan colt put in his care, and I guess that convinced him to stay on. When did he go missing? Just since the sale?"

"No, more than a month ago," I answered.

He grimaced. "Nobody tells me anything. I'm managing the stallions here. The yearlings aren't my responsibility, so I didn't even go to the sale—though I heard the Trojan colt brought a hell of a price. Still, if he runs up to his pedigree, I suppose it might be worth it someday."

"Someday?" I repeated.

"Selling for three million and change is one thing. Winning it on the track is another."

"So I've been told," I said. "Anyway, you hadn't heard from Billy Paulson since he told you he was staying at Mill Creek?"

Chessman chuckled again. "He didn't tell me," he replied. "Maybe he thought I'd bite his head off. He had a friend deliver the news. I sent him a New Year's card to show there were no hard feelings, but I never heard from him again." He sighed. "They come and go awfully fast in this end of the business."

And not always of their own volition, I thought. Aloud I said, "Thanks for seeing me, Mr. Chessman . . ."

"Hal," he interrupted me.

"Thanks for seeing me, Hal," I amended. "I appreciate your taking the time."

"Not a problem," he answered. "If you see Billy, tell him I'm not mad at him."

"Will do."

"And drink your coffee, or Diablo will have a fit," he concluded with a smile.

"I'd forgotten all about it," I said. I took a taste, found it was getting cool, and drank it down like a glass of water. "Tell him he makes a good cup," I added, getting to my feet and placing the cup on the tray.

"I'll walk you to your car," he said.

"If you've got work to do . . ." I began.

"We have the sex Olympics morning and evening," he responded. "In the afternoon we rest."

"You breed them twice a day?" I said, surprised.

He nodded. "When there's a demand for it. Around here, just Pit Boss and Marauder. And then, of course, no girlfriends for half a year. Can't have a September or October baby turn a year old a couple of months later. Though even that's changing."

"You're breeding mares toward the end of the year?" I asked.

"Not here," he replied quickly. "But some of the popular studs do double-duty, standing the first half of the year here or in Europe and the second half in Australia. They made a hell of an offer for Trojan, but the syndicate voted against it. They decided he's too valuable to risk."

"How come?" I asked, though I was pretty sure I knew.

"Man's made some bad investments. Even bounced a couple of pay-checks. That Trojan colt was his salvation, and he didn't want even the notion of twice as many Trojans coming to market, even halfway across the world, to lower the winning bid by a penny."

"What did he do to make his money in the first place?" I asked.

"He was born," was the answer.

"That's all?"

"And he was 4-F."

I frowned. "I don't quite follow that."

"Rich parents, two kids, both boys. One was 4-F, the other got killed in Vietnam. Parents die. Presto: instant millionaire. Not as rare in this business as you'd think." He smiled. "It's not a sport for the mildly wealthy."

"When did his fortune start going downhill?" I asked.

He shrugged. "I'm sure his wife would say it was the day he bought Mill Creek. Truth to tell, I don't know. He still runs the damned place, so he must have some money left . . . and now he's got three million and some, minus Fasig-Tipton's commission."

He made sure none of the help were around as we approached my car. "My own opinion is that he'd have gone belly-up last year if he hadn't sold his share of Trojan, though of course I can't prove it. I think he stayed in the syndicate just long enough to get that colt and vote against standing Trojan in Australia, and then he cashed out."

"What's a share worth?"

"Whatever you can get for it," he replied with a smile. "Shares in Seattle Slew originally went for three hundred thousand. When he turned out to be an even better sire than he was a racehorse, a couple changed hands for over four million apiece."

I let out a low whistle. "That's remarkable!"

"Don't be too impressed. For every sire whose value multiples ten or fifteen times, there are fifty who'll never be worth as much as the day they were syndicated. Today there are probably twenty stallions within thirty miles of here who syndicated for ten million or more and now have a market value of two million or less."

"It sounds like Monopoly money," I said.

"They spend it like Monopoly money too," replied Chessman. "The trick is not to go to jail instead of passing Go and collecting your two hundred dollars—or two hundred million, in this business."

We reached my car, and I turned and shook his hand.

"Thanks for your help, Hal," I said. "And your private guesswork remains just that: private."

"Nice meeting you, Eli," he said as I got into the car. "And remember to give Billy my best if you run into him, and tell him I'm not mad."

"I will," I answered, starting the motor, while a little voice in the back of my head say: Don't hold your breath.

18.

I drove around for an hour or so, just letting the scenery relax me as I tried to clear my mind, which was too damned cluttered with useless details. Then I started getting hungry, and I remembered that I'd promised to take Bernice out to dinner. Well, to *meet* her for dinner anyway.

I drove back toward the station, passing another one along the way. It was nice to know they had so many cops on duty, but the place was so peaceful I couldn't help wondering why. Then the answer hit me—to keep the place so peaceful, of course—and I realized that I really was getting tired.

I stopped by the motel to take a quick shave and shower, put on a clean shirt—no noticeable dirt on the one I'd put on in the morning, but I had a feeling it and I both smelled of horses, or at least of stables.

Finally I drove to the station and walked up to Bernice's desk.

"You ready?" I said.

"In about five minutes," she said. "My replacement just got here, and she's in the washroom changing."

"Into what?" I asked in a feeble attempt at humor.

"We're not plainclothes detectives like some people I could mention," she replied. "When we're on duty, we have to be in uniform." She checked her watch. "She should be here in the next minute or so."

"Then what do we need five minutes for?"

She gave me the kind of look I'm sure an owner gives a lame horse that he just bought an hour earlier. "I have to get back into my civilian clothes."

"Sorry," I said. "I've been concentrating too much on trillion-dollar horses and not on beautiful policewomen."

She smiled. "For a compliment like that, all is forgiven."

A graying blonde in freshly pressed police blues approached us. "I'll take over now," she said.

"Fine," said Bernice, getting to her feet. "Eli, this is Brenda. I'll just be a couple of minutes."

"Hello," I said.

"Hi, Eli," replied Brenda. "I feel like I know you already. You're almost a resident here at the station from what I hear."

"Too bad I'm not," I said. "It's cleaner than most of the places I've been this week."

She laughed. "That's the first rule of the game in horse country: Watch your step."

"I'd rather be James Bond, wearing a tuxedo and sitting across elegant gaming tables from master criminals," I replied. "But I can't tie a bow tie, and I've never found a pair of patent leather loafers."

She smiled at me. "Bernice was right," she said. "I like you already."

"Bernice said you'd like me?"

"She said you were likeable."

"I hope she still thinks so after dinner," I said.

"I hope for your sake she still thinks so," said Brenda. "We police-women are tough."

"I'll treat her with all the respect due a member of the law."

"You'd better," answered Brenda. "She doesn't brag about it, but she's the best shot in this station."

Bernice joined us then, looking not beautiful, she hadn't been beautiful even twenty years ago, but very pretty and immaculately groomed and dressed.

"Did I give you enough time to tell Eli a bunch of lies about me?" she asked pleasantly.

"She told me how you won the war—she never mentioned which one—and I told her how I brought jazz up the river from New Orleans," I said.

"I see both of your noses have had time to shrink back down to normal," replied Bernice. She turned to Brenda. "Hold the fort until Phil gets here. See you tomorrow."

"Phil? I asked as we walked out the door to my car.

"He's got night duty on the desk this month," she answered.

"So you work the desk by day?"

"This month," she replied. "It rotates."

"And the rest of the time?"

"Oh, a little of everything," she said noncommittally. Then she smiled. "I'd advise you to resist the urge to rob a bank when I'm not busy being the desk sergeant."

"Damn!" I said. "I guess I'll be late on my rent next month."

She laughed as we reached the car. "Where are we going?" I asked as I opened the door for her.

"Not too far," she said. "I want to make sure this car can get us there and back."

"It may not look like much," I said, "but it's dependable." Except when it isn't.

"Kind of like you," she said. "Well, what kind of food do you like?"

"Got any Greek restaurants in town?" I asked. "I love pastitsio and dolmades and saganaki."

She just stared at me.

"This is Lexington, Eli."

"Italian?"

She nodded. "That can be arranged." She directed me, and in about three miles we pulled up to a little restaurant at the edge of a small strip mall that had a sign proclaiming that it was Antonelli's.

We entered, and a young man who looked more Hispanic than Italian led us to a table along a side wall. She ordered wine, I ordered a Bud, and we spent the next few minutes looking over the menu. I finally hit on veal parmesan, and she chose some kind of fish dish I'd never heard of and couldn't pronounce.

"You'll like the food here, Eli," she said when the waiter, who also didn't look Italian, disappeared into the kitchen to deliver our orders.

"Do you come here often?" I asked. "Or just when you're on a Dutch treat date?"

She laughed. "Once or twice a month. I eat most of my meals out."

"Makes sense. Why slave over a hot stove after a hard day of paper-work or arresting baddies?"

"We have our share of drunks and druggies and the like," she said. "But what really interests me—and it's all taken care of at higher levels, usually by the feds since it invariably crosses state lines—are the machi-nations of all the self-proclaimed royalty of the horse industry."

"Is there all that much going on?" I asked.

"Not that you can prove, though now and then we get a headline case. But you know, when there are maybe fifty farms valued at twenty million or more, and a couple of hundred horses with market values in eight and occasionally nine digits, it's difficult for everyone to observe the niceties of the law."

"Yeah, I can imagine," I said.

"Anyway, it makes the paperwork interesting," she continued. "For example, you're looking for a young man who worked for Travis Bigelow, and that's probably as far as it goes—but wouldn't it be fascinating to know how a man who inherited something like fifty million dollars and could buy Mill Creek outright, without a mortgage, managed to blow just about every penny he owned?"

"It's not exactly a secret that he's been having financial troubles," I said.

"I know. But how do you blow that kind of money?"

"Beats the hell out of me," I replied. "I worry more about how I can blow fifty bucks on a weekend. Besides, the flip half of the business is just as curious."

"I don't follow you," she said.

"Take two horses that look pretty much alike. Stand them side by side. Call the one on the left Old Plodder. Call the one on the right Trojan. Both are retired from racing. Neither has ever had any off-spring make it to the track yet. But one of them is worth two thousand dollars, probably to some dog food company, and the other's worth maybe fifty million today, and that could triple or quadruple in six or seven years if his foals start winning some major races." I paused, while she tried to see what I was getting at. "Bernice," I continued, "there are entire countries—or at least well-populated sections of them—

that don't have an annual gross domestic product worth as much as Trojan. Five or ten million kids will starve to death this winter. Now I'm sure Trojan is a nice, well-behaved animal who loves his groom, doesn't dirty his stall, and breeds mares on command—but when all is said and done, he's just a horse. What makes a dumb animal worth that kind of money?"

"I'm sure you expect me to say fools like Bigelow, who shell out that kind of money for a surrogate to win what they haven't won, or perhaps to consider themselves sportsmen, whatever that means—but you know, the average two-dollar bettor is just as guilty. The tracks return about three-quarters of everything that's bet, pay upkeep and taxes on the rest, and still have enough left over to shell out hundreds of millions in purses. And the guy who's betting his welfare check, or putting off his child support payment so he can lay some bets, is just as guilty as the guy who buys two percent of a top stallion for a million dollars."

"I bow to your superior knowledge," I said.

"You live in Blue Grass country, you learn about the industry," she replied. "I grew up in New York City, where the average musical play costs ten million to put on and lasts less than a week. What makes one crazier than the other?"

"A telling point," I said. "At least finding lost kids and putting bad guys in jail makes sense."

"How long have you been doing it, Eli?" she asked as the waiter arrived with our salads.

"I started out as a cop, a uniformed cop, in Chicago. Moved up to the detective bureau after half a dozen years."

"And?"

"And arrested the wrong people."

She frowned. "The wrong people?"

I nodded. "Stalwart reservoirs of the public trust," I said. "They came out of it okay. After all, they owned half the lawyers and all the judges, and I was on my way to Cleveland. Things didn't work out any better there: I shot a guy who was shooting at me, I lost my job, and my wife left. I got tired of getting fired for doing what I was paid to do, so I came to Cincinnati about five years ago, maybe a little less, and set up shop as a private eye."

"She left you because you shot a man in self-defense?" she asked.

"I think it was more because I was unemployed again," I answered wryly.

"Mine left for someone fifteen years younger, fifteen pounds lighter, and an inability to stop giggling," she said. "I keep hoping he'll turn up in the drunk tank, but with her at home he doesn't go out much."

"By God," I said as the waiter took our salads away, "I just love trading stories with another winner."

She laughed so hard I thought she might actually fall off her chair. Somewhere about thirty seconds into it I got the distinct impression that she was suddenly crying, but she pulled out a handkerchief, wiped an eye, and pasted a smile back on her face.

"So," she said, changing the subject, "are you getting any closer to finding your young man?" she asked. "His parents check in every day to see if we've turned anything up."

I shook my head. "No, he's still thoroughly missing."

"Any ideas?" she asked as the main courses arrived.

"We can discuss it after we eat."

She nodded. "So you think he's dead?"

"I didn't say that," I replied.

"You didn't have to," she said with another smile. "Someone raised you to be a gentleman, Eli. Oh, you can't tell it from the way you dress or some of your language, but you hold doors open for me, you held my chair for me, I could tell it hurt you to agree to a Dutch treat, and now you're putting off talking about the young man because dinner's arrived and you don't want to upset my delicate feelings." She leaned forward. "I'm a cop, Eli. Such delicate feelings as I may still possess are compartmentalized and only come out when I'm alone. So shall we talk?"

"Did I really pull out your chair for you?" I said. "I wasn't even aware of it."

"Yes, you did."

"Son of a bitch!" I said, and then looked up toward the ceiling. "Thanks, Ma."

"So why do you think he's dead?"

"Nothing that'd hold up in court or even hold water if you argued that he's still alive," I said. "Anyway, his car's still here."

"That's the only reason?"

I shook my head. "These aren't exactly reasons. They're feelings, notions, suspicions. I can't forget the way he looked the last time I saw him. He was at least very worried and quite possibly very scared. He was going to talk to me in the morning. Same thing with his girlfriend. He talks to her in late afternoon or early evening, tells her he's got a serious problem and he'll speak to her about it in the morning, and he never shows up." I took a bite of my veal. "Not bad," I commented.

"It's quite good," she said. "I've had it before." She paused and stared at me. "There's something else. I can tell."

"A couple of things," I said. "First, why the hell did he drive his car across town and park it in a Kroger lot with the top down when it had been raining and was due to rain most of the night?"

"Good question. Which Kroger?"

"Leestown Road."

"Interesting," she said noncommittally. "What was the other thing?"

"Eddie Arcaro's riding crop."

She blinked and frowned. "I beg your pardon?"

"Billy Paulson was Tyrone's groom until about six weeks ago."

"Tyrone?" she asked.

"The Trojan colt that Tony Sanders was caring for. Anyway, Billy went AWOL too. Vanished just as quickly and just as thoroughly as Tony."

"What has this got to do with Eddie Arcaro's whip?"

"According to Hal Chessman, who hired him at Mill Creek last year, that was Billy's most cherished possession. He even kept it tucked in his belt or in a boot all day while he worked."

"Okay," said Bernice, "it was his most cherished possession."

"And he left it behind when he disappeared. And Tony left his car and his girlfriend."

"I'd hardly call her a possession."

"I agree, but the car and Nan—that's her name—are two things he cared for very much."

"More than anything, like the other kid and the whip?"

"I don't know," I said, thinking back on Tony's love for all aspects of racing and breeding. "But why leave them behind? More to the point, if he wasn't going to need the car, why not sell it? Why let it sit in the rain with the top down?"

"So you don't think they'd leave without the whip and the car, and they haven't shown up here," she said. "From this you conclude that they're dead?"

"I don't conclude anything," I said. "But it's sure as hell a possibility."

"I agree that it's a possibility," said Bernice. "But of course there are others, too."

"I'm open to suggestions," I said, digging into my veal parmesan. "Damn, this is great stuff! Thanks for suggesting this place."

"Okay," she said. "Suggestion Number One. You say they each were the groom for Errol—"

"Tyrone," I corrected her.

She shrugged. "Same thing. Pretty boy with a sword. Only Basil Rathbone knew how to use the damned thing. Anyway, they both cared for this wildly expensive colt. Maybe a potential bidder paid them for inside information about him."

"What kind?"

"I don't know. Maybe he has sore knees. Maybe something about his mouth will make it impossible for a jockey to restrain him once his blood is up. I'm just talking possibilities. Maybe he paid them and told them he didn't want them around until well after the auction."

I shook my head. "Why pay them both, if he could get the information from one of them. And if Tony's hiding on bribe money, why hadn't he called his parents or his girl. He has to know how worried they are."

"Why do kids do anything?" she replied. "Anyway, I'm just offering suggestions."

"Got any more?"

"Maybe they really are frustrated beach boys at heart."

"Not the type," I said.

She made a face. "That's what they all say."

"Really, I don't buy that for a second."

"Okay," she said. "Tyrone had a mean streak—an erratic one that doesn't show up often—and put the first kid in the hospital. Tony found out about it and didn't know whether to go public with it since the colt was being auctioned the next day, and if Fasig-Tipton forced him out of the sale, Bigelow might go bankrupt and Tony would feel it was all his fault."

"A lot of *couldas* and *mightas*," I said.

"If it was easy you'd have solved it already, Eli," she said. "Lou checked you out. You're damned good at your trade."

"Then why am I always broke?" I shot back.

"One has nothing to do with the other," she replied. "You're a good detective. You're a lousy businessman."

I couldn't argue with that, so I grunted an acknowledgment and finished my main course while she did the same.

"So," I said as the waiter took our plates away, "you want dessert?"

She shook her head. "You go ahead, Eli. I'm trying to lose a little weight."

"You look fine."

She smiled. "And your mother would have taught you to say that even if it was the biggest whopper you told all day."

"If my nose doesn't grow, it must be the truth," I replied.

"I'll skip it anyway," she said.

"So will I then."

I signaled for the check, the waiter brought it, and I grabbed it before she could see it.

"How much do I owe you?" she asked.

"A friendly good-night kiss will cover it," I said.

"Really," she said. "I mean it."

"So do I," I said, digging into my wallet and slipping the waiter a pair of twenties. "Keep the change," I told him, which didn't sit too well with him since the bill was for thirty-six dollars and ten cents.

I ushered Bernice out to the car before she could leave a couple of dollars on the table, then had her direct me to her apartment.

"Somehow I thought of you living in a house," I said as I walked her to the front door.

"I used to," she said. "But it was just too much work, holding down a job and keeping the place up. I don't know that I'm any happier here, but I'm a lot less exhausted." She turned to me and put her arms around my neck. "Thanks for dinner."

We kissed, and then she opened the outer door. "See you tomorrow?"

"Probably," I said.

"We could do this again if you're still in town."

"It's a date," I said.

Then she was inside, and I walked back to the Ford, started it up, and began driving back to the motel. I was about halfway there when I noticed that a Mercedes convertible with very bright headlights was tailgating me, so I slowed down and gave it room to pass.

It roared up, and just as I thought it was going to jump ahead of me it lurched to the right and gave me a hell of a bump, running me off the road. The shoulder was no more than ten feet wide, and it was all I could do not to careen into a drainage ditch. I finally pulled to a stop, got out, walked around the car to assess the damage, and decided that it had been a long day, the car could get me to the motel, and I'd worry about fixing it in the morning.

And since I had friends in the Lexington police force, I'd also report a Mercedes with a driver who was probably higher than a kite.

19.

When I got into the room I turned on the television to see how the Reds were doing. Not too well. They were down five to three in the seventh inning.

At least Lexington wasn't so caught up in the horse industry that nothing else mattered. I remember that once I was on a case—a runaway boy, and that one had run away—that took me down to Midland, Texas. The president gave a speech to the nation that night. Preempted all the networks' programming to do it. And when I picked up the newspaper the next morning, the first three pages were listings of new oil drillings, and the president's speech was on page 4.

The hotel had cable, so I ran through about fifty channels until I found an old Michael Shayne movie with Lloyd Nolan. They'd probably made it in under two weeks, and it was still more enjoyable than ninety percent of the junk they charged you ten dollars a ticket for these days. I concluded that either I was getting older or the public was getting dumber; probably a little of each.

I decided I could use some coffee. The room didn't have a coffee maker, and I probably wouldn't have known how to use it anyway, so I took an inside corridor to the office, where they had a big pot on hand, poured myself a cup, added the requisite white stuff, and looked around for something to see after Michael Shayne finished making with the wisecracks and finally brought the bad guys to the bar of justice.

There were some giveaways promoting local attractions, a few of which didn't even involve horses. There were out-of-date copies of Time, which told you why the Iranians weren't really a threat; Fortune, which told you how to get (almost) as rich as Steve Forbes; and Cosmopolitan, which told you how to enjoy eighty-three—count them:

eighty-three—different sexual positions with the man of your choice. (I assume it was aimed at women—and wildly creative women at that, or at least acrobatic ones.)

Somehow none of those magazines appealed to me, and I was about to go back to the room when I spotted a copy of Thoroughbred Weekly— I still had a couple dozen issues of it in my trunk waiting to be delivered to Tony's parents—and I figured what the hell, at least I don't have to be an Iranian, a millionaire, or a contortionist to read it, so I picked it up and went back to my room with the magazine and the coffee.

Michael Shayne was just about through with the jokes, so I waited for the denouement (which wasn't anywhere near as interesting as the rest of the film), watched him go into a clinch with the girl who would prove to be his one true love (until the next film), tried to find some music to read by, couldn't find anything but rock (which bears about as much resemblance to music as I bear to Clark Gable), and finally shut the damned thing off.

Then I settled down in the room's one easy chair with my coffee and my magazine and started thumbing through it. It was a couple of weeks old, which probably made it the newest publication in the motel. Most of the issues I'd seen in Tony's possession had photos of major races on the covers, but evidently the Keeneland summer sales trumped even that, because here, two weeks before the sale, was a photo of the sales pavilion with a handsome young yearling posing there with his groom. The caption announced that this was the previous year's sale topper, but they were expecting at least three yearlings, including the first Trojan colt ever offered at auction, to beat that price.

I started reading the ads—every major yearling got a full page— and when I came to Tyrone's ad I felt like a friend of the family. I knew that horse, had actually rubbed his muzzle, had his name and his scar explained to me. Tony wasn't in the picture—none of the grooms were in any of the photo ads—but you could tell that he was just off camera to the right, that Tyrone was posing just the way Tony had worked with him. And I thought: if you're as good as your pedigree, maybe someday I'll be standing at the rail cheering you home in a major stakes race.

I also saw an item that Mill Creek Farm would be dispersing most of their broodmares. Frank Standish had to know that, but he was a loyal employee and hadn't mentioned it to me. I decided he'd be looking for another farm to manage within a year. Or maybe he'd even stay at Mill Creek, if Bigelow could find an angel to buy it from him.

I continued thumbing through the magazine, which, if it did nothing else, impressed upon me the scope of the business. There were fifteen or twenty pages reporting the most recent stakes races. Forty or more pages of ads for stallions and at least that many for the upcoming yearling sale. There were bloodstock agents advertising for clients, farms advertising for help, tracks bragging about their purse money in the attempt to attract horses and trainers, even a few farms for sale. The one thing it didn't have was any ads for betting systems; clearly the industry knew that while betting supported it, it was a losing proposition. I even remembered Harry Sixth Street and Arlington Benny back in Chicago constantly explaining that, yeah, you could beat any particular race, but what no one could do was beat the races.

I set the magazine down, tried the television again, same channel, and found myself halfway through a Boston Blackie movie. Chester Morris was no Lloyd Nolan, but I didn't hold that against him. After all, I was no Sam Spade or Philip Marlowe. They dealt in murders; I looked for lost dogs and lost kids.

Eventually Blackie got his man, I went to the office and got another cup of coffee, and I came back to the room. This time the Saint— not the Roger Moore Saint, but his grandfather, the George Sanders Saint—was out to rid the world of evildoers. I figured Charlie Chan and Mr. Moto were probably next, and I turned to one of the ESPN channels, where I got to watch a thrilling minor league baseball game from somewhere in Arizona.

I left it on, with the sound way down, walked over to the desk, sat down on the hard wooden chair, and pulled a sheet of Motel 6 stationery out of the desk's drawer. I'd been on the case for a few days, and I thought I'd see what I'd managed to learn.

I began writing down names:

Frank Standish
Jeremy somebody
Travis Bigelow
Hal Chessman
Nanette Gillette
Billy Paulson

And though I didn't have a name, I added: Someone or someplace near the Leestown Road Kroger.

Then I looked at what I had and began making notes.

Standish: *Was he in the barn while I was at dinner? I doubt it. Did he have anything to gain by Tony's disappearance? No. Were they friends? Not to my knowledge, but more to the point, they weren't enemies.*

Jeremy somebody: Just a groom in Standish's employ. The only motive I can think of, and it's a damned silly one, is that he was jealous of Tony and wanted to be in charge of Tyrone—but that's crazy, since Tyrone was selling the next afternoon.

Travis Bigelow: He's got so many problems on his hands, and such a big operation, I'd almost be surprised if he knew Tony by sight. And what the hell could a kid like Tony know that could possibly harm or threaten Bigelow? They just didn't operate in the same world.

Hal Chessman: He was gone four months before Tony was hired. They probably never even met, since neither went to the track.

Nanette Gillette: She cares for him, she misses him, she seems genuinely concerned that he's missing. More to the point, what possible motive could she have? This isn't a marriage. If she wants to break it off, she just says "Good-bye."

Billy Paulson: He's missing too, and that Arcaro whip makes me think he either left in a huge hurry, like maybe in fear of his life, or that he didn't leave at all. But either way, it's got nothing to do with Tony. It's doubtful that they ever even met.

Someone or someplace near the Leestown Road Kroger: Leaving his car there with the top down is the best reason to assume he never left town—but no one seems to know anyone in the area or think he knew anyone. There are no horse farms, no nightclubs, no nothing. To borrow a line from Yul Brynner: Is a puzzlement.

I stopped writing and picked up my coffee cup, only to discover that it was empty and probably had been for the past half hour. I picked up the sheet of paper, walked over to the easy chair, sat down, and stared at it.

Was there anything I was missing? More to the point, was there anyone I was missing?

I couldn't come up with anyone. The kid lived a pretty restricted lifestyle. He spent most of his time at the farm, even slept there, and when he got a spare hour or two he drove over to visit his girlfriend. Maybe he saw his parents at church on Sundays. I hadn't asked, but it sure as hell wouldn't put them on my list. After all, they were paying me to find him.

The only other person I could think of was the guard at the track, the one who ushered me over to Barn 9 and who seemed to know Tony, or at least who he was. But that was crazy. Not only couldn't he have had a motive, but he also didn't have time to kill the kid without driving the horses wild, stash the body, and cover up all signs of it when I'd be returning from dinner in half an hour, and more to the point, when any potential buyer might stop by unannounced at any second.

I stared at that paper, and stared at it, and finally I crumpled it up and threw it in the wastebasket. Hell, maybe the kid had flown the coop and was frolicking with half-naked beach bunnies on the sands of South Beach. Maybe I'd been a detective too long, been lied to too many times by too many people that I just couldn't accept the obvious anymore. Maybe I'd give it one more day of driving around talking to people who'd already told me everything they knew, and then tell Tony's parents that they were wasting their money.

I turned on the television again, saw Charlie Chan saving Number One Son yet again—I'm a trained detective, right? I knew he'd be on next—and turned it back off.

Then I got up, stretched, and realized that I was wide awake. Probably I'd had too much coffee, or maybe it was too few results, but whatever it was, I wasn't ready for bed. I remembered a sign at Tilly's that they were open around the clock, even if Tilly had to sleep now and then, and I decided to drive over there for a little snack.

I opened the door and saw movement in a blue Mercedes convertible that was parked across the lot. Then there was a flash of light—I never heard the bang!—and a bullet thudded into my door about two inches to the left of my ear.

I dove to the floor and kicked the door shut, reached up and turned off the light, and crawled to a window. I moved the curtain just enough to peek out and saw the Mercedes racing out of the parking lot.

Clearly it hadn't been an accident or a drunk driver before. Somebody was out to kill me, and since I was a stranger in town, it had to be because of the Tony Sanders case.

But what had suddenly made me a threat—and to whom? What the hell did I know now that I didn't know yesterday?

20.

I waited about five minutes until my heartbeat and blood pressure returned to normal, peeked out through the curtains once more to make sure the Mercedes was gone, and then called Drew MacDonald.

"What's the matter, Eli?" he said. "You sound kind of tense."

"I'm calling from my motel," I told him. "Somebody took a shot at me."

"You're sure?"

"Damn it, Drew—this isn't the first time I've been shot at!"

"All right, all right. Who was it?"

"I don't know. Some guy in a blue Mercedes convertible. The top was up, if that helps. The son of a bitch tried to run me off the road earlier tonight."

"Well, he obviously knows where you're staying. I'll send a couple of boys in blue out in a squad car to bring you in."

"Good," I said.

"This has something to do with the missing kid, right?"

"I can't think of anything else it could be," I said.

"You going home tomorrow?"

"To Cincinnati?" I said. "Hell, no! I want to know who's shooting at me, and why, and I want you guys to lock him away."

"I figured as much," he said. "Can I make a suggestion?"

"Go ahead."

"Pack your bag, pull anything out of your car you might want, and bring it all with you—but let the cops drive you. Leave the car right where it is. We'll put you in protective custody at the jail overnight, and after we identify his car, or fail to, we'll rent you a car and set you up in a different motel. And in the meantime, I'll post a plainclothesman at your motel in case this guy comes back."

"Sounds good to me," I said. "I won't leave the room or go out to my car until your men get here."

"Shouldn't take five minutes," he said. "You sure you're okay?"

"Yeah, I'm fine. But my gun's in my glove compartment, and just between you and me, I probably couldn't hit the broad side of a barn from the inside."

"Any idea why he started shooting at you now?" continued MacDonald. "What did you dig up today?"

"That's what's driving me crazy," I said. "I didn't learn a damned thing."

"Clearly somebody thinks you did."

"Clearly somebody's wrong."

"Go over everything you did, everyone you spoke to, everything you saw. Maybe you'll figure out what he thinks you know. I'm going to hang up now, Eli. I've got to send some cops to your motel. I'll see you in a few minutes, when they bring you in."

"See you then," I agreed and hung up the phone.

I tossed all my clothes, clean and dirty alike—I hadn't brought that many—into my beat-up leather bag, added my toothbrush and shaving kit from the bathroom, and sat down to wait for the cops.

It didn't take that long. In about four or five minutes there was a knock at my door—the one leading to the cars, not to the interior corridor. I opened it, and two tall, slim, uniformed men—one white, one black—stepped in.

"Mr. Paxton?" said one of them.

"That's right."

"Lieutenant MacDonald said you were expecting us," he continued. "I'm Officer Crosby, and this is Officer Graham."

"I'm glad to see you," I said. "Did either of you notice a blue Mercedes convertible in the lot?"

He shook his head. "We were specifically told to look for one."

"Good," I said. "Then just let me get a couple of things out of my car, and we can go to the station."

"One moment, sir," said Graham. "We understand you were shot at when you opened the door to go to your car?"

"That's right."

"I didn't see any damage to the door. Was the shooter directly facing you?'

"No," I said. "He was off to left."

"Okay," he said. "Then if the door was open, the bullet should be . . ." He walked over to the wall. "Ah! Here it is." He turned to me. "Officer Crosby will help you empty your car. Forensics is overloaded right now, so I'll dig it out myself and they can run it through the lab." He grimaced. "At the rate they're cutting budgets, I'll be washing squad cars next month."

"This way, Mr. Paxton," said Crosby, ushering me out the door as Graham went to work on the wall.

I walked to the Ford, and he held my bag while I opened the trunk. There was nothing there except Tony's back issues of the racing magazine. I figured I'd see his parents before I saw the car again, so I picked them up and tucked them under an arm, then closed the trunk, pulled my pistol out of the glove compartment, tucked it in a pocket, and followed Crosby to the police car, where Graham joined us a minute later.

We drove directly to the station, where Brenda—Bernice's counterpart—checked us in and directed us to a room where Drew Mac-Donald was waiting for us.

"Thanks, guys," he said, taking a tissue and wiping a spot from his glasses. "I'll take it from here."

They nodded, handed him the bullet in an evidence bag, and left the two of us alone.

"Any idea yet who it might have been?" he asked.

I shook my head. "None." Then, "Damn it, Drew—I haven't learned a goddamned thing! I'm no closer to finding the kid now than I was when his parents hired me."

He smiled. "Yes, you are, Eli," he said. "You just don't know it."

"Same damned thing," I replied.

"No, it's not," said MacDonald. "If the kid ran off to have a good time, no one would be shooting at you."

I nodded in agreement. "You're right. I'd pretty much convinced myself that Tony was dead, so that didn't register. But before it was guesswork. Now I have a valid reason to believe he's dead."

He held up the small plastic bag with a misshapen bullet in it. "We'll have the forensics boys—well, actually the forensics ladies at this station—examine your valid reason in the morning. If they can't make a positive ID, they'll probably send it on to the state lab."

"See if you can see who owns a blue Mercedes convertible too," I said.

"Did you get a look at the license plate?" he asked.

"It was dark and he was shooting at me."

"I'll take that for a No," he said. "That's too bad. Still, we can draw a couple of conclusions."

"Such as?"

"The shooter's probably not local—or if he is, he rented the car. I mean, how the hell many blue Mercedes convertibles can there be in a city this size? I'll put the computer to work on it, and I'll have a list of every one of them in three minutes' time."

"Okay," I said. "So what do I do now?"

"We'll rent you a car in the morning and find you another motel, something really grubby and off by itself."

"You make it sound like you're paying for it."

"I wish we could," he said, "since you're doing some of our work for us, but Cincinnati detectives aren't in our budget. I'll have them roll in a cot with a blanket, which you won't need, and some pillows, which you also won't need but will probably appreciate. That door there leads to the bathroom." He paused. "If you're as tight for money as most independent private eyes are, hell, you can use this room as a headquarters."

"I'll think about it," I told him.

"Okay," he said, walking to the door. "You want some coffee, or are you going to go right to sleep?"

I shook my head. "It's only been twenty minutes or so since someone tried to blow my head off. I'll need a little more time to calm down, so, yeah, a coffee would be nice."

"I'll be right back with it."

I didn't see any reason to unpack my suitcase, so I set it down on the floor, sat down at the little table that was across the room from where they were clearly going to put the cot, and started thumbing through Tony's pile of Thoroughbred Weekly magazines.

A uniformed guy, one I hadn't seen before, wheeled a cot into the room and opened it up. I felt like I should tip him, but I controlled the urge and just thanked him instead. He saluted, which may have been the first time any cop had saluted me since I left the Chicago force, and almost bumped into MacDonald as he left.

"Your coffee," he said, placing it on the table next to the magazines. "Cream and sugar, right?"

"White stuff—cream, milk, half and half, powdered creamer, whatever," I said. "And half—sugar, Sweet and Low, Equal, you name it."

"I thought all detectives drank their coffee black," he said with a smile.

"I thought all detectives made it with an oversexed blonde or redhead every night," I replied, returning his smile. "Looks like we were both the victims of false doctrine."

"By the way, I ran a check on the Mercedes," said MacDonald. "Got to be out of town."

"Are you seriously suggesting that no one in this town owns one?"

"No. I'm seriously suggesting that based on the list of owners, no one who's remotely connected with either the horse or the murder business owns one. I'll have one of our men drive around tomorrow looking for fresh marks."

"Marks?"

"You say he bumped you off the road," he said. "Can't do that without leaving some scratches and dents, no matter how good you are at it."

"I'd just about forgotten," I admitted. "Funny how being shot at half an hour ago can make you forget what happened three or four hours ago."

"And this was after you dropped Bernice off at her place?"

I nodded. "Right."

"Well, he didn't pick you up out of the blue. He must have followed you from the station to dinner, and from the restaurant to her apartment." He grimaced. "Smacks of a pro. He doesn't give his employer a freebie, especially a cop. He knows that if he nails one of us, we'll never quit until we track him down."

"I can't tell you how comforting that is," I said with a smile, "knowing you'd never give up if he'd shot at Bernice instead."

"We don't want to lose you either, Eli," he said. "Did you remember your gun?"

"Yeah, it's in my pocket."

"With the safety on, I trust?"

"Hasn't been off in something like two years."

"Got some bullets too?"

"Whatever's in the gun," I said, "and maybe fifteen more."

"That's not a hell of a lot."

"Oh, come on," I said. "If my first ten or twelve shots don't kill or disable whoever's after me, how the hell many more do you think I'm gonna have time for before he nails me?"

MacDonald laughed. "Now I'm going to spend the rest of the night wondering whether you're a realist or a fatalist."

"As long as I'm a live one, I'll settle for either," I told him.

"Okay, Eli," he said. "I really have to get back to work. You're not locked in and are free to walk around if you want. Don't go through the doorway at the left end of the corridor. It's the drunk-and-drug tank, and they've pretty much shut up for the night. I'd hate to get them all screaming again."

"Right," I said.

"I'll check on you in the morning before I go home and see if there's anything you need and what you've decided to do."

"I appreciate it, Drew," I said.

Then he was gone, and I sat down at the desk, opened one of Tony's magazines, and started reading about how the Trojan offspring would dominate the two-year-old races next year if they ran half as well as they looked. There was a nostalgic article about the first yearling to sell for more than one hundred thousand dollars, which was considerably less than the average price of the past thirty years. They named him One Bold Bid, and he ran about the way the cognoscenti expected any sales topper to run, which is to say, he retired without ever winning a stakes race.

There was an article about Trojan himself. Evidently he was breeding about one hundred and fifty mares a year, and from a photo they ran of him I'd say he was putting on a little bit of a belly, which made no sense to me. I mean, if I slept with a hundred and fifty women during the last six months of the year, there wouldn't be enough of me left to weigh.

I read every word and looked at every picture in the two most recent issues, and then that cot started looking very inviting, so I walked over to it and lay down. I thought I'd probably lay awake for an hour or two, trying to figure out my next move, but I was asleep within a minute and didn't budge until Lou Berger woke me just before noon.

21.

"Drew filled me in about your little problem," said Lou Berger as I swung my feet to the floor and sat at the edge of the cot.

"Little?" I growled.

He smiled. "Misshapen little piece of lead. Can't be much more than half an inch long."

"So what did it tell you?"

"That it was shot by a guy who didn't register his gun," was the answer.

"Big surprise," I said.

"So what are your plans?"

"Someone wants me dead. The only two things I've done since I got here are guard a horse and look for a kid. The horse is probably a thousand miles away by now, so I figure I'm being shot at to stop me from looking for the kid."

"So . . . ?"

"As far as I can see, there are only two ways to make this guy leave me alone. Run back to Cincinnati and hide there, or find the kid before he can kill me."

"Well, there's a third," said Berger. "But we'd have to arrest you, though you'd probably beat the charge."

"Not interested," I answered. "I'm no hero. If I lived in Seattle or Boston, I'd be on my way home the minute I walk out of this building. But Cincinnati's just ninety miles up the road, and if I go home now there's no guarantee that he won't be there tomorrow, or even this evening, because until the kid turns up alive or dead the hitter has no reason to stop trying to kill me. So I'll try to find Tony before he finds me."

"We'll help you in any way we can," said Berger seriously.

"I'm counting on that," I said. "Let me start with a request: I'd like to spend the next couple of nights here at the station."

"Well," he said dubiously, "I suppose it saves money, but still . . ."

"It's not about the money, Lou," I said. "Hell, I'll pay for the space if you want. I just want to be able to sleep for a few hours without worrying about what might be sneaking up on me."

"Not a problem," said Berger promptly when he realized what my reason was.

"Just leave my junk in the room here," I said.

"Toss out the magazines?" he asked. "I see Mars Rover on one the covers. He hasn't won a thing since February down in Florida, so it's got to be at least three months old, and probably four."

"No, leave 'em here," I answered. "They belong to Tony. I'll be dropping them at his parents' place today or tomorrow."

"So where do you go first?"

"Beats me," I said. "I just woke up a couple of minutes ago." I reached for my pack of cigarettes, then realized I'd left them in the Ford. "We got any coffee around here?"

"Yeah. It's brewing on the shelf between the two bathrooms."

"Thanks." I let myself out of the room, plodded down the corridor to the men's room, made brief use of it, and then poured myself a cup of coffee and added powdered creamer and sweetener. I took a sip and then a swallow, started feeling mildly human again, and walked back to Berger's office, where he had just seated himself at his desk.

"Did you turn up anything on the convertible?" I asked.

He shook his head. "There are eleven blue Mercedes convertibles in town, and we've accounted for every one of them. There's only one for rent, and it wasn't out yesterday. So clearly it was from out of town, and if it was rented by our friend from New Mexico or any other hitter, he probably picked it up in Kansas or Iowa with a phony ID so we couldn't trace it to him."

"If it was Jimenez and he didn't mind being seen here the night Tony vanished, why would he mind it now?"

"You're still sleepy, aren't you, Eli?" said Berger. "Or at least your brain is."

"Probably," I agreed. "But enlighten me."

"He wasn't shooting at anyone until last night."

"Oh," I said dully. "You're right: I am too sleepy to think. If I'm leaving this particular safe house, I'd better finish this coffee and start waking up."

"I assume you know how to take care of yourself once you're awake," said Berger. "But I think we'll put a plainclothes tail on you, just to be on the safe side."

"As long as he doesn't spout political slogans while he's gunning down the bad guys."

"Are you still sleepy, or do you have reason to think there's more than one?"

"Still sleepy," I said. "Where can I pick up some breakfast or lunch when I leave here?"

"Can't do any better than Tilly's," said Berger.

"I don't think so," I said. "If the shooter's been watching me, he'll know that I like to eat there. My Ford's at the hotel, and it's like driving around in a bull's-eye, so if you can get me a different car, I'll go some-place I haven't been and maybe grab a meal without being shot at."

He thought for a moment. "There's a bunch of Bob Evans restau-rants here in town. Pick one that's not too close to the station or Big-elow's farm and you should be all right."

"Thanks," I said. "Now all I have to do is figure out why I'm a target."

"You could visit every place you've been the past couple of days," he suggested. Then he shook his head. "No, that wouldn't prove a thing. He's already shooting at you, so if he follows you to places that have nothing to do with his reason, it won't prove anything."

"If it's all the same to you, I'd just as soon not be shot at," I said.

"Then you're going to have to turn into Sherlock Holmes and solve this by pure deductive reasoning, because the second you visit Bigelow or Standish or the kid's parents again, you're a target again, like it or not. You might not know why he's trying to kill you, but he sure as hell knows, and that means you've already given him his reason."

"I know," I said. "But that's crazy. I've talked to a couple of trainers, a couple of grooms, a couple of parents, and a girlfriend. Nobody knows anything. I'll stake my life on it."

Berger sighed deeply. "In case it's escaped your notice, you already have."

"It doesn't make any sense," I complained. "They answered everything I asked. Nobody ducked, and I know if I'd had lie detectors on them they'd all have passed."

"Has it occurred to you that maybe you didn't ask them the right questions?"

"What do you mean?"

"Just that no one tried to kill you three days ago, or two days. All you've done is go around asking questions. Maybe if you'd asked the right one, you'd know why you've become a target."

"That makes sense when you say it," I said. "But what the hell else could I have asked?"

"Beats me," said Berger. "I wasn't there. But clearly he thinks you know something you shouldn't know."

And an hour and a half later, when I put aside the sports section of the Lexington paper and finished my third cup of coffee to go along with my second cheese Danish at a Bob Evans a dozen miles from the station, I still didn't know.

22.

I suppose what it came down to is that I had more confidence in the shooter than I had in myself. Which is to say, I was sure he hadn't made a mistake, and that means I had—if not a mistake, at least an error of omission. There was something I should have asked that he figured a competent detective would have asked, and the answer to it, or possibly the mere fact that I knew enough to ask it, was reason enough to kill me.

I had no leads at all on Tony's disappearance, or Billy Paulson's either . . . and in fact, if the two were linked it was by the most improbable of connections, that they both rubbed the same horse.

Well, maybe that wasn't the only link. They'd both worked for Mill Creek. Maybe they'd each learned something, maybe even the same thing, about Bigelow, something he didn't want anyone to know, something that could put him in the poorhouse even quicker than he seemed to be heading for it.

Of course, that would mean that these two uneducated kids had discovered something that no one else in Bigelow's employ had hit upon, and while he wasn't surrounded by geniuses, he'd had a couple of pretty competent managers in Chessman and Standish. I knew he had an accountant, and he probably had maids and butlers. I'd met one of his gofers; there had to be more. It was difficult to think that only Tony and Billy had the pure deductive powers to unearth whatever it was they had unearthed.

After another four cups of coffee, I got the distinct impression that if I ordered one more she'd pour it on my head to open up the table to better-paying customers, so I got up, left her a five-spot so she wouldn't throw a coffee pot at my head as I walked past, paid my bill, and climbed into the Chevy that Berger or one of his officers had rented for me.

Then I just started driving around, still dwelling on the problem, and realized I was wasting the Sanderses' money if I didn't go somewhere and do something, though I was a little vague on where and what. But I knew I couldn't just keep driving until the light dawned, so I went back to Mill Creek Farm, parked near the barn area, walked around the backhoe, and found Frank Standish walking from the yearling barn; it still housed a bunch of colts and fillies, as only the very best-bred of them had been accepted for the Keeneland sale. He was heading to the large barn that housed his office.

"Another leak?" I asked, indicating the backhoe.

He nodded. "If Mr. Bigelow keeps this place much longer, I think he's going to have to replace every pipe on the property, plus half the barns. What can I do for you, Eli?"

"I've hit a bunch of dead ends. I thought I'd take another look around and see if I missed anything."

"You've got free run of the barns and paddocks," replied Standish. "If you want to go to the Big House—that's what we call the Bigelow residence—I'll have to get permission, but I can't imagine anyone will say no, especially with Mrs. Bigelow off visiting friends in Manhattan."

"No, if Tony didn't spend any time there, I don't have to."

"Truth to tell, I don't think he ever once set foot in the place."

"Where did he spend most of his free time?"

Standish smiled. "There's not a lot of free time to be had when you're working with animals, Eli."

"He couldn't spend twenty-four hours a day with Tyrone," I protested.

"Of course not. But he had other yearlings as well."

"He did?" I said, surprised. "I thought he just cared for Tyrone."

Standish shook his head. "You ship the most expensive horse on the grounds to a sale, you ship the groom he's used to with him. The others learn to adjust to new grooms in a day or two, but you never want the money horse left alone in strange surroundings."

"How many other yearlings did he care for?"

"Two colts and a filly. They're still here."

"He's not planning to race them?"

Standish shook his head again. "He hasn't raced a horse in fifteen, sixteen years. He'll be selling these. They just weren't good enough in either bloodlines or conformation for Keeneland in the summer."

"There's more than one sale here?" I asked.

"Yeah," said Standish. "What just finished was the Select Summer Sale, the very best-bred and best-conformed yearlings. There'll be three or four times as many at the fall sale, but they won't bring the kind of prices the summer yearlings did." He paused to signal a girl to take a broodmare to a certain pasture. "The interesting part is that the fall sales are every bit as likely to produce a classic winner as the summer sales. It just won't be quite as well-bred to start with."

"To start with?" I asked.

"Obscure Stallion X sires a Derby winner and a Santa Anita Handicap winner, and suddenly he's Hot Stallion Y. Breeding's not quite the science we wish it was. There's a centuries-old saying that still holds true: Breed the best to the best and hope for the best."

"That's fascinating," I said, "but I'm getting sidetracked here. Let me rephrase my question: On those incredibly rare occasions when Tony wasn't working his tail off, where did he hang out?"

"Mostly with his girlfriend, I think," said Standish.

"I mean when he was here," I said. "Like if he took a half-hour break and then had to go back to work. Where would he take it?"

"Ah!" he replied with a smile. "Now I understand. You see that little room there, just down from my office?"

"I thought it was an equipment room."

"A tack room?" he said. "It is, but Tony turned one end of it into a reading room."

"He didn't strike me as a bookworm," I noted.

"There was one subject that fascinated him and that he knew very well."

"Horse racing," I said with certainty.

He nodded. "He subscribed to most of the magazines. We get them here, of course, but he subscribed long before he came to work. But we've got quite a library of books—a complete run of the annual

American Racing Manual, lots more—and he used to sit in there whenever he had a chance and read them."

"May I take a look?" I asked.

"Be my guest."

I walked down to the room. It was dark, of course, but I found a light switch just inside the door. I'd half expected to see shelves of books there, but it was mostly grooming equipment, extra buckets, and horse blankets and the like—and in one corner was a swivel chair on wheels that someone at the house no longer wanted and had given to the barn area, and an abandoned lamp with a rusty base. I tried it, and it still worked.

I looked around for a few minutes, found three hardcover books in a cardboard box—all on racing, of course—but nothing else. There wasn't a damned thing to be learned here that would make someone want to start taking shots at me.

I went back into the main aisle of the barn, couldn't see Standish anywhere, and went outside looking for him. I found him about fifty yards away, leaning against a split-rail fence watching a half dozen broodmares and their foals cantering across the grass. I couldn't figure out why the mares were running—maybe something startled them, or maybe, because they'd been race mares, they just felt an occasional compulsion to run—but the foals were clearly having the time of their very young lives.

"Beautiful, aren't they?" I said as I walked up to him.

"Esoterically," he agreed. "But practically, the smaller bay doesn't stride out enough, and some trainer's going to go crazy trying to teach the roan to switch leads."

"Switch leads?" I asked. "I don't know what you mean."

"A horse, even a Secretariat, gets tired if he leads with the same foot all the way around the track," Standish explained. "Ideally, since they run counterclockwise, you want him leading with his left foot on the turns and his right foot on the straightaways. I know it doesn't sound like much, but it'll make the difference of a length or more in a six-furlong race . . . and a lot of races are won—and lost—by less than a length."

"I didn't know that."

"No need for you to. You're not a trainer or a jockey."

"Is this the pasture where Tyrone ripped up his neck?"

"I sure as hell doubt it," said Standish. "I just got here in January, and I gather he slashed it in September or October. But it wouldn't have been this paddock."

"Why not?"

"Too small. Those weanlings like to run, so it would have been one of the two big ones"—he pointed at the paddocks in question—"off by the weanling and yearling barns."

"You don't have a vet on the grounds," I said. "How did they patch it up before he bled to death?"

"It's only about ten or twelve inches, and he doesn't have any arteries right there," said Standish. "They tell me they just called the vet, held him still for twenty minutes 'til the vet arrived, and got him sewn up. Didn't even anesthetize him. Of course, we don't have the facility to knock a horse out and work on him here anyway. Probably they made a value judgment that it was easier to patch him up right here in one of the barns than send for a horse ambulance, take him to the vet's hospital, and put him under before they tried to stop the bleeding. He's a pretty tractable colt; he'll let you do almost anything with him."

"Did Tony ever say anything about him?" I was grasping at straws, but I couldn't think of any other question.

"Just his daily reports."

"On what?"

"The usual: Did he clean out his oats? Did he have any open sores? Was he snorting too much (which might imply a breathing problem when he got to the track)? Things like that."

I felt myself getting tense and nervous. There was someone out there, still intent on killing me, and not only hadn't I learned a damned thing, I couldn't think of another question to ask.

Finally I just thanked him and walked back to the Chevy. As I drove away I checked every driveway I passed, every cross street, looking for a blue Mercedes convertible. The fact that I didn't see one didn't make me feel any better. All it meant, as far as I was concerned, was that the shooter was skilled at arranging ambushes.

23.

I stopped at Fishbein's, walked in, and looked around for Nanette. She was nowhere to be seen. My first thought was that she knew something, and the killer got to her. My second thought, far more rational, was to ask the cashier where she was. I was informed that she was on her break and would be back in a couple of minutes.

I wandered over to the magazine section and realized that I didn't have to exert the usual willpower, as Fishbein's didn't carry Playboy or its imitators. I saw a Raymond Chandler paperback, picked it up, thumbed through it, and wondered why Philip Marlowe (or Sam Spade, or Lew Archer, or any of the other fictional detectives) never seemed to feel nervous when someone was out to kill them. Or why each had, at most, one friend on the police force that he could trust and rely upon.

I put the book back and began walking up and down the aisles, not looking for anything in particular, just killing time. Finally, as I was studying a package of disposable baby diapers, I felt a tap on my shoulder, resisted the urge to jump, resisted an even stronger urge to pull my gun, and turned around to find myself facing the lovely young blonde.

"You wanted to see me, Mr. Paxton?" said Nanette. "Is there some news about Tony?"

"Not yet," I said.

She frowned. "I'm very worried about him."

"I know," I said, doing my best to sound comforting. I'd have put an arm around her shoulders, but I had a feeling that could get you arrested in a family drugstore in the Upper South.

"You obviously have more questions to ask," she said. "How can I help you?"

"This one's out of left field," I said, "but do you or Tony know anyone who drives a Mercedes convertible?"

She shook her head. "That costs what one of us makes in maybe two years," she answered. "We don't travel in those social circles."

"Like I said, it was a long shot," I replied. "Do you know if Tony ever worked for a guy—a farm manager—named Chessman?"

"No. He mentioned him now and then, always favorably. I guess he worked for Mr. Bigelow but left before Tony started."

"Only one more question, and this is an important one," I said. "Unfortunately, it's also an inexact one. Did he know or even mention anyone who might live in the vicinity, say two or three blocks, of the Leestown Road Kroger?"

She frowned. "I don't think I've ever been there. Did someone there see Tony?"

I shook my head. "No. And it has nothing to do with the Kroger itself. I just need to know if he knows someone who lives or works near there."

"I've no idea, Mr. Paxton, but I can't imagine that he does. He's always been pretty much of a loner. I'm sure if he knew anyone in that area, he'd have told me about it."

I must have shown my disappointment, because suddenly she looked even more worried.

"If you'll tell me who you think he knew there," she said, "I'll be happy to help you look for them every day when my shift's over."

"I wish I knew," I admitted.

She frowned. "Then why are you asking me about it?"

I figured it couldn't hurt to tell her the truth. "Because the police found his car parked there." I decided not to tell her that he'd left the top down with a rainstorm coming.

I promised to keep her informed of any developments and then walked out to the Chevy, which I'd parked right in front of the store, got in, and tried to think of what I might have missed. Finally I decided to drive back to Keeneland.

It was a lot less crowded now that the sale was over, and it wouldn't be open for racing again until the fall, but there were still about fifty or sixty cars parked there—trainers, exercise boys (well, that's the term, though half of them are girls these days), grooms, track officials, the crew that maintained the track, and a couple of unclassifiables.

I walked over toward where the yearlings had been stabled, and as I approached Barn 9 a guard approached me.

"Excuse me, sir," he said. "May I see your credentials?"

"I'm just looking for someone," I replied. "Another guard, in fact."

"Even so, I'm afraid you're not allowed in this area without a pass."

"My name's Eli Paxton," I said, pulling out my wallet and flashing my detective's license. "I just want to see the guard who was on duty here during the sale."

"We had lots of guards," he replied, relaxing somewhat now that he saw I was almost a cop.

"I need the guy who was in charge of Barn 9."

"I'll have to go check the duty chart," he said. "I can't leave you here alone, so why don't you come with me, Mr. Paxton?"

"Lead the way," I said, falling into step behind him as he walked to a small building at the end of the row of barns. We entered it, and while I was looking for a chart tacked to a wall, he activated a computer, typed in a few words, waited for an answer, and then turned to me.

"The man who you want is Roger Combes," he announced. "He's currently at"—he peered intently at the screen—"the owners' and track officials' private lot."

"And where is that?" I asked.

"Under the clubhouse," he said, pointing toward the grandstand. "Just a minute." He pulled out an official-looking notepad, scribbled something on it, and handed it to me. "This'll get your car in and save you walking almost a mile each way from where your car is now. We're not racing, so Roger should be the only one on duty today."

"Thanks," I said. "Much appreciated."

I walked back to the Chevy, got into it, and drove where he had indicated. I finally pulled into the private lot, and as I got out of the car, Combes walked over.

"May I please see your—?" He stopped dead and stared at me. "Don't I know you?"

I nodded and extended my hand. "Eli Paxton. I was keeping watch over the Trojan colt."

He smiled. "Ah! Now I remember. And he topped the sale, didn't he?"

"Yes, he did."

"Pretty horse." Suddenly he frowned. "Ah! I remember now. That groom went missing. That's why you're here, isn't it?"

"As a matter of fact, it is," I said.

"He seemed like a good kid. It's hard to believe that he just ran off to have a good time before the colt even made it to the sales ring."

"A lot of us are finding that difficult to believe," I replied, "which is why I've been retained."

"Good!" he said.

I stared at him curiously.

"I'd hate to think nobody cares."

"People care," I said. "His parents, for starters."

"So what can I do to help?" asked Combes.

"The night before the colt was sold . . ." I began.

"The night the groom disappeared," he interrupted, nodding his head.

"Right," I said. "I was with him all day, and again at night. The only time I left the barn was to eat at the kitchen. Now, think hard, because this may be very important: Were there any visitors during the half hour or so I was gone for dinner?"

"We don't keep a record of each visitor, Mr. Paxton," he said. He closed his eyes and seemed to make almost a physical effort to concentrate. Finally he opened his eyes and looked at me. "I think he only had one—a portly gentleman with white hair."

"Do you know who it was?"

He shook his head. "No. It was probably just a potential buyer or his agent or trainer. Whoever it was, he had a right to be there. He spent a few minutes talking to the young man, probably asking questions about the colt, and then he left."

"And that's all you can remember?"

"I seem to think he was local, that I may have seen him a couple of times over the years, but that's all," said Combes. "I'm sorry, Mr. Paxton. If I'd known then that it was important . . ."

"Not your fault," I said. "And the likelihood is that it was just a possible bidder and had nothing to do with Tony's disappearance."

"When he finally turns up, let me know," said Combes. "He was a nice kid. Whenever he wasn't working he was always reading. You just don't find many young people like that."

"I agree," I said. "Well, thank you for your time, Mr. Combes."

"Roger," he corrected me.

"Roger," I amended.

I walked back to the Chevy, pulled out of the parking lot, and realized I had no idea where to go next. I could visit his parents, or Standish, or Nanette, or Chessman, or Jeremy the farm hand, or even Bigelow himself, but the truth of the matter is that I was all out of questions to ask them—and I was no closer to finding out what had become of Tony Sanders than the morning I woke up and found that he was missing.

24.

I awoke to the smell of coffee and saw Bernice standing there in the doorway with a tray that held a pot, a cup, and the necessary white stuff.

"Well, look who finally woke up," she said as she walked into the room and put the tray on a table.

"Coffee in the hands of a good-looking woman does it every time," I said, swinging my feet down to the floor and sitting on the edge of the bed.

"So is Sam Spade making any progress?"

I shook my head. "Not so's you'd notice it."

"Let me know if there's anything I can do to help," she said.

"If I can come up with something, you'll be the first to know."

"There's always the possibility that he just ran off, you know," she said. "Thousands of kids do, every month."

"I know," I said. "I just don't think he's one of them."

"Drew went home an hour ago," said Bernice. "He didn't have any messages for you. Lou's in his office if you need to speak to him."

"Thanks," I said. "Let me inject some of that coffee into a vein first."

"Okay," she said. "I'll be at my desk if you need me."

I poured the coffee, stopped by the bathroom, considered shaving, decided I was still groggy enough that I might slit my throat, and went back to finish the coffee. I thumbed aimlessly through one of Tony's magazines. After a few minutes I started feeling a little more human as the second cup took effect, and walked over to Berger's office.

His door was ajar, and he was hunched over his computer, reading some report on the screen.

"You open for business?" I said.

He swiveled around on his chair. "Hi, Eli. Come on in."

"Thanks."

"So what can your local police department do for you today?" he asked.

"Not much, to tell the truth," I said. "I've got just one thing left to do, and if it doesn't work I'm going to tell Tony's parents not to waste any more of their money."

"An honest private eye?" he said with a smile. "You'll destroy the whole profession's reputation."

"I can make up for it by promising the moon to the next woman I take out," I said, returning his smile.

"Not Bernice," he replied. "I don't think there's enough money in petty cash to pay for your funeral."

"Then I'll just lie to the IRS like everyone else does," I said. "Of course, first I have to make enough for the IRS to give a damn."

"Don't count on that. They'll come down on you just as hard for a nickel as a million." He picked up a coffee cup from his desk and took a sip. "Okay, how can I help you?"

"Yesterday I went to Keeneland," I said. "I hunted up the security guard who'd been in charge of some of the barns at the sale, including the one where Tony and I stayed." I felt a need for a cigarette, looked around, couldn't spot an ashtray, and tried to ignore the craving. "I asked him if there'd been any visitors during the half hour I was over at the kitchen having dinner, and he says there was just one."

"That's awfully thin, Eli," he said. "The horse was on display to anyone with credentials, and that included every registered buyer and trainer on the grounds."

"I know, I know," I said. "But trust me, the kid was happy and care-free when I left, and he acted like he had the weight of the world on his shoulders when I got back thirty minutes later."

"Okay," he said, frowning. "Go on."

"I asked about the visitor. He couldn't remember the name, but he was sure it wasn't one of the nationally known trainers like Wayne Lukas or Bob Baffert that even I would recognize from their photos in the sports section. So I asked Combes—that's the guard—to describe him, and he remembered that he was kind of fat with a head of white hair."

"A fat guy with white hair," repeated Berger with a smile. "Well, that eliminates half the men and all the women."

"It's a long shot," I agreed. "But damn it, Lou, something spooked that kid while I was gone."

"So to come back to it, what do you want me to do?" asked Berger.

"You must be able to print out a photo of this Jimenez. I want to see if Combes recognizes it."

"I seem to think he's an elegant, well-built guy, kind of a 1930s ladies' man, with coal-black hair," said Berger. "But who knows? Maybe he's overeaten and gone gray. I can get the photo faxed to us in five minutes' time."

"Thanks, Lou," I said.

"Tell you what," he added. "There's always a possibility that Horatio Jimenez is back in Albuquerque with a dozen friends who will swear he hadn't left town for a century, so let me also give you photos of some local muscle that probably wouldn't be adverse to threatening the kid or taking a shot at you if the price was right." He finished his coffee and turned back to his computer. "Hell, maybe one of them is even a fat guy with white hair."

He began pounding away on his keyboard, then turned back to me.

"Okay," he announced. "Give it three or four minutes, and they should show up right there." He pointed to his fax machine.

"Thanks, Lou. I hate to keep imposing on you, but . . ."

"Not a problem," he said. "That's what we're here for." Suddenly he grinned. "Though if this goes on for another week, we may ask you to contribute to our pension fund."

"If Combes can't identify any of the photos, this doesn't go on past dinnertime," I told him.

We tried to kill a little time while waiting for the photos, but he didn't know who was playing for the Reds or the Bengals, and I didn't know who was playing for Kentucky's basketball team, which he persisted in calling "Big Blue." We finally found a sporting figure of mutual interest—Trojan—but just about the time we began discussing him, the first of the photos arrived, and shortly after that, two more showed up.

"Okay," he said, "these are all I sent for. Their names are at the bottom of the pictures. Here's your boy Jimenez."

He handed it to me, and I studied it. Jimenez looked to be somewhere around forty, showing just a little gray on his sideburns, with an elegant black mustache. He looked like the romantic lead in a black-and-white movie—not any particular one, just a generic one—and what he sure as hell didn't look like was a fat guy with white hair. Still, there may have been two or three visitors while I was gone, and Combes might have remembered only one off the top of his head.

I put the picture aside and studied the other two. One was fat and mostly bald, the other looked like eight million guys you'd pass on the street and never give a second thought to.

"All right," I said, getting to my feet. "Let's see if any of these can jog Mr. Combes's memory. And thanks again."

"Don't thank me," he said with a smile. "Thank the Lexington taxpayers."

Then I was out of his office and heading toward the front door.

"Are you coming back in time for dinner?" asked Bernice.

"Yeah," I said. "But probably just to pick up my suitcase."

"So you figure either you'll have licked it or it'll have licked you by the end of the day?" she asked.

"Something like that," I said.

"Well, I'm off at five if you want cheering up at dinnertime," she said.

"I appreciate that," I began, "but . . ."

She held up a hand. "I know what happened after you dropped me off the other night."

"And it doesn't bother you?" I asked. "It sure as hell bothers me."

"Of course it bothers me that they're trying to shoot you," she said. "But we could take my car and go to a different part of town."

"If I decide to stay, I'll take you up on it. And thanks."

She laughed. "When you're forty and divorced, you don't wait to be asked."

"I appreciate it," I said "When you're my age and divorced, you get out of practice."

She laughed again, and then I was out in the parking lot looking for a blue Mercedes convertible and thankfully not seeing one. I climbed into the Chevy, hit the ignition, and headed over to Keeneland for what I was sure would be the last time.

I reached the track, pulled into the clubhouse lot, and went looking for Combes. It didn't take me long to find him.

"Good morning, Mr. Paxton," he said. "I didn't expect to see you again, at least not so soon. What can I do for you today?"

I walked up to him. "I want you to take a look at this"—I handed him the faxed photo of Jimenez—"and tell me if this was the man who visited Tony Sanders and the colt while I was having dinner."

He looked at the photo and instantly frowned. "No, sir, Mr. Paxton. Not even close. The man I saw was heavyset, and he had a full head of white or maybe gray hair."

"How about this one?" I said, showing him the fat bald guy.

He shook his head. "No. Even with white hair the features are wrong."

"Okay," I said. "I don't have much hope for this one either, but you might as well take a look."

I handed him the final fax. He just looked briefly and shook his head again.

"I'm sorry, Mr. Paxton, but I never saw any of these men," Then: "Well, let me amend that. I could have seen all of them in a shopping mall or a basketball game or even in church. They have pretty forgettable faces, except for the one who looks a little like Zachary Scott, if you remember the old movies. But I know that none of these three came to visit the groom that night."

"Okay, Mr. Combes," I said, taking the faxes back. "I'm sorry to have troubled you."

"No trouble at all," he said. "I'm just sorry I wasn't able to help you."

"You and me both," I said wryly.

I shook his hand and walked back to the car.

And that, I thought, was that. I'd run through every possibility—I hesitated to think of them as leads, because "lead" was more definite than anything else about this case. There was nobody left to talk to, and if there was a question left to ask, I couldn't think of what it might be.

I checked my watch. It was already eleven, so since I was charging Tony's parents for a full day, I figured I owed them another five or six hours. Then I'd pick up my luggage, go out to dinner with Bernice, swap the Chevy for my Ford, and go home and tell my troubles to Marlowe, who would show his opinion of my reappearance by chewing on my best shoes.

25.

I considered my options, not that I really had any. I could drive out to Mill Creek Farm again and talk to Frank Standish, but that hadn't helped the last few times I'd tried it. I could go back to the track and see if I could get Combes to remember anything other than that the visitor, who may or may not have had anything to do with Tony's disappearance, was fat and white-haired. I could talk to Nanette again, but it was obvious that she knew even less about the situation than I did.

I could barge into Bigelow's house and accuse him of murder and/ or kidnapping, and if he didn't fall over laughing after I tried to prove it, the next night I spent in the police station I'd have a door and window with bars in them.

I could talk to Hal Chessman again, but he was gone from Mill Creek months before Tony arrived and had never seen him.

Those were my choices.

Still, I felt guilty just going back to the station, sitting around playing solitaire or reading racing magazines and waiting for Bernice to clock out so I could have one last dinner with her before I went home to Cincinnati.

I decided to think about it at lunch and see if I had any remaining options. I'd just driven up to a sandwich shop that looked like a clone of Tilly's when it occurred to me that I wasn't the least bit hungry, that I'd talked myself into stopping because I didn't know what the hell to do next.

I ran through them all in my mind again—Bigelow, Standish, Nanette, Combes, Chessman—and knew seeing any of them again would be fruitless. Finally I decided to drive back and take a second look at the Leestown Road Kroger, or rather the area immediately around it, and see if I'd missed anything the first time.

It was useless, I knew, but I had a few hours to kill, and it beat sitting at the station feeling like a total failure, so I headed over there.

The parking lot looked exactly the same as last time. I peeked into the store as I slowly drove by the front; it looked as clean, as well-managed, and as inviting as before. I stopped to let a young man pushing a dozen empty carts go by and watched him take them into the store.

I drove twice around the lot, couldn't see a thing that looked suspicious or out of place, drove around the back where the huge eighteen-wheelers delivered the products that Kroger sold. It seemed as quiet and well organized as the front. I'd have asked the guys on the loading dock some questions if I could think of any to ask, but of course I couldn't.

Okay, no surprises, and at least I'd killed half an hour while going through the motions. I spotted a nice little restaurant and decided I'd drive once around the area, just to complete my wasted quest in this part of town. Then I'd grab some lunch while I decided how to kill the rest of the day.

I began driving south a couple of blocks, turned at a minor cross street—and then I saw it, parked between a pair of condos: a blue Mercedes convertible. The top was up, and there was a guy inside it, reading a newspaper. I slowed down and tried to get a look at him. His face was buried in the paper, and when I reached the corner I took a right and began circling the block. When I was directly opposite it on the next street, I stopped, pulled out my pen, and reached into the glove compartment looking for a piece of paper. All there was, except for a pair of maps, were the rental papers, which had been signed by Berger and billed to the cops. I put them in my left hand, held the pen in my right, and started driving again. This time I slowed down about thirty yards behind the convertible, read the plate, and began scribbling it down while I weaved down the street at a snail's pace.

A guy behind me honked, but that didn't worry me. Even if the hitter in the convertible looked over to see what the fuss was about, all he'd see was a green Chevy he'd never seen before.

As I passed him I put my hand up as if shielding my eyes from the sun so he couldn't get a look at my face. That was my mistake. The sun had ducked behind a cloud, and it took him less than a New York second to figure out I didn't want him to see who I was.

He pulled out, honking at the guy who was behind me and directly in front of him, and I took off like a bat out of hell. I was doing sixty in a few seconds and hoping some squad car would show up to arrest me, but as the saying goes, there's never a cop around when you need one.

I hit a wall of traffic and had to slow down, and suddenly he was right behind me. He didn't know who I was—he hadn't seen my face and I wasn't in the Ford—but he knew I was interested in him, and that was enough. I could see his hand and arm come out the driver's window, and I heard a shot, though none of my windows broke.

I saw signs for I-75 south to Florida and I-64 to Louisville, but I figured the last thing I wanted to do was race my little 6-cylinder Chevy against a sleek Mercedes, so I kept turning into the city, looking for heavier traffic and more turns.

I had to slow down when some lady on my right, plugged into her cell phone and paying no attention to anything, ran a light that had just turned red for her and green for me. There was another shot, and this time my back window shattered.

I turned into an alley and floored it. He was slow reacting, but the Mercedes made up for it once he entered the alley, and he was almost on top of me when I turned right onto another street.

The next cross street was a commercial one, going one way to the right, with a light at the corner. I ran the light and took a left, going into the one-way traffic. There were a bunch of cars coming at me. They honked like hell, but they jogged left and right to avoid hitting me.

The Mercedes swung into the street right on my tail. He stuck his arm out and took two more quick shots. I felt one thud into the trunk, and the other shattered the window of an oncoming car. I swerved and barely avoided him, and an instant later I heard a crash behind me. I checked the rear-view mirror and saw that an SUV that had barely avoided me had side-swiped the Mercedes. No one seemed badly hurt, but the SUV had spun around and was blocking the street, so that was the end of the chase. I saw the Mercedes' driver jump out of his car and dart between two buildings.

I turned again at the next street, with the traffic this time, started to get my bearings—I'd been so intent on escaping that I had no idea where I'd been driving—and finally made my way back to "my" police station.

Bernice got up from her desk the second I walked in the door.

"Are you all right, Eli?" she said solicitously. "You look terrible!" She glanced out the door. "What happened to your car?"

"Everything in order," I said. "But the very first thing is this: there was a car crash"—I gave her the general location; I couldn't remember the street or any of the numbers—"and no, it didn't involve me. Well, not exactly. But the shooter in the blue Mercedes was involved. No one was driving away from that, so there had to be a cop on the scene in a couple of minutes. The shooter ran off, but I got his license plate number." I handed it to her. "See if the cop got a description of him from any witnesses. And warn any cop who's looking for him that he's armed and dangerous."

"Lou's in conference and Drew hasn't come in yet," she said. "I'll take care of it myself. Sit down somewhere, Eli. You look terrible."

"I'd say that you ought to see the other guy," I said wryly, "but the whole exercise is about finding out who the other guy is and why he wants me dead."

"We don't have any medics here," she said. "But go into the bathroom and clean the blood off. We've got bandages there."

"Blood?" I repeated, frowning. "What blood?"

"Just go," she said, starting to type on her keyboard. "You'll figure it out."

I went to the bathroom that was attached to the room I'd been staying in, turned on the light, and peered into the mirror—and found that I was bleeding from my right ear and two spots on my right cheek. I hadn't felt it in the heat of the chase, but the shot that shattered the window had sent some slivers of glass against the right side of my face and cut it open.

I checked the cabinet, found some anti-bacteria spray, closed my right eye and sprayed it on my face, then stuck a couple of bandages on.

The ear bled right through, so I covered it with two more, one on top of the other, and that seemed to do the trick.

When I went back out to Bernice's desk, she already had the information.

"Well?" I asked.

"It looks like you were right. Or maybe it was Lou who suggested it. Anyway, the guy in the blue Mercedes matches Horatio Jimenez's description." She paused. "What the hell happened, Eli?"

"The son of a bitch tried to kill me again."

"Why?"

"I wish to hell I knew," I said. "A week ago I'd never heard of him, and I'm sure he'd never heard of me. I'm no closer to knowing what happened to Tony Sanders than I was the minute his parents approached me—and yet he's tried to kill me twice." I sighed and shook my head. "I'd give my kingdom, such as it is, to know what he thinks I know." I paused a moment and thought about it. "Hell, I don't even think he knew it was me. I was in a different car, and I don't think he got a decent look at my face."

She frowned. "Then why was he shooting at you?"

I thought about it, and then thought about it some more. "It doesn't make any sense, does it?" I said at last.

"Did he mistake you for someone else?" asked Bernice dubiously.

"No, he couldn't have," I answered. "Not unless we assume he was waiting to kill some guy who drives a two-year-old green Chevy."

"What was he doing in his car when you spotted him?"

"Taking a break, staking it out, waiting for a friend, who the hell knows?" I answered with a growing sense of frustration.

"That doesn't make any sense, Eli," she said.

"Name me one thing about this case that does," I shot back.

"Well," she continued, "there's one positive aspect about this whole mess."

I stared at her. "I'd love to hear it."

"There is a solution, and you must be very close to it," said Bernice. "Otherwise, why would they have tried to kill you?"

"Like I just said, I don't know for a fact that he knew it was me."

"He knew it was you after you took me home from dinner," she said. "And even if he didn't recognize you today, he was parked there, and he didn't shoot the first hundred or so cars that drove past." She stared intently at me for a moment. "Oh, shit! You're bleeding right through that bandage on your ear."

She summoned another uniformed policewoman, who arrived about half a minute later.

"Eli, this is Officer Hutchinson, but you can call her Jeanine. Jeanine, this is Eli Paxton. He's been staying with us the past few nights, though I don't think you've met him. Right now he's concentrating on bleeding all over himself and also on our nice clean floor. Would you please take him somewhere and clean him up properly, and see if you think he needs to see a doctor?"

"I'll be happy to," said Jeanine. "It beats listening to the guys talking about who should and shouldn't be starting for Big Blue this fall." She turned to me. "Follow me, Mr. Paxton."

"Call me Eli," I said.

She smiled. "You may not feel so friendly after I finish working on that ear." She peered more closely at me. "Your cheek doesn't look all that good either."

She led me to a small lab—not forensics, not anything in particular, just a little room with a bunch of computerized equipment and a hell of a lot more supplies than the bathroom's medicine cabinet.

"I'll be as gentle as I can," she said, "but this is probably going to hurt."

She pulled the bandages off my ear, and I couldn't stop myself from grunting in pain.

"Bad guys, or just careless in the kitchen?" she asked as she began cleaning the wound a lot more thoroughly than I had.

"One or the other," I said.

"Hey, I'm one of the good guys."

"A guy took a couple of shots at me while I was driving, and shot out a window."

"Yeah, I thought so," she said, picking up a small metal tweezers. "Your cheek seems to be okay, but you have a little sliver of glass in your ear lobe." She very carefully pulled it out. "How clever of you to tape it in so I could see it for myself."

"Anything to please a cop," I said, suddenly wincing as she touched something tender with the tweezers.

"Sorry," she said. "It's out now." She began applying some kind of salve. "All done. Don't wear your earrings tonight."

"I'll resist the temptation," I said.

She continued looking at the earlobe. "I think exposure to fresh air is best for it. You've bled all over your collar and shoulder already, so you can't do much more damage to the shirt." She stuffed some cotton and a bandage in a plastic bag and handed it to me. "If it starts bleeding again, use this."

"Thanks, Jeanine," I said when she backed off to indicate she was all through patching me up.

"I've got two sons," she replied with a smile. "This is old hat to me."

We walked back to Bernice's desk, I thanked her again, and she vanished into the inner recesses of the building.

"Lou says he'll catch up with you—I think his exact words were 'I'll debrief him'—in about forty-five minutes. Maybe he can figure out what Jimenez was doing there." She paused. "We can still go out to dinner if you're up to it—and if you have a clean shirt. If you feel you'd rather skip it, that's okay too."

"We'll go," I said. "Even potential murder victims get hungry."

"And are you still going back to Cincinnati tonight?"

"Hell, no," I said. "I don't know what I've missed that they think I know, but they've tried to kill me twice, and I'm damned well going to find out why."

Her computer started beeping, and a minute later an officer brought in a man who'd been drinking way too much way too early in the day, and I could tell I was in the way, so I went to "my" room, lay back on the cot, and tried again to dope out what they thought I knew that warranted my death.

26.

Lou Berger came into my room in about half an hour.

"I hear you've had an exciting day," he said.

"And it's only half-over," I replied wryly.

"You want to tell me exactly what happened?"

I recounted everything from when I drove to the Kroger and how I managed to get away from my pursuer.

"That was quick thinking," he said. "Quick, but dangerous. I don't think I'd have gone the wrong way into traffic."

"You would have," I said, "if the guy behind you was shooting at you."

"Maybe," he admitted, and then added: "Especially based on the descriptions we've got."

"I know," I said. "It was Jimenez."

"Looks like. We can't be sure, but it figures. What we can't figure out is what the hell he was doing there. I checked, and not a house or condo on that block has changed hands in more than a year."

"I don't know," I said. "Hell, you could fill a book with what I don't know about this case." I pulled a pack of cigarettes out of my shirt pocket. "Sorry," I said as I lit up. "I need this."

"Terrible for your health," remarked Berger.

"Not as terrible as getting shot at by a pro," I said, taking a deep drag. "I don't suppose anyone's found him yet?"

"Eli, the guy had a gun in his hand, and he'd been shooting at you. Do you really think anyone followed him?"

"No," I admitted. "Hell, I wouldn't have either."

"You might have," he said. Then he smiled. "But you'd have checked to see if there was a reward first." He stared at me for a long moment. "So are you staying on the case or going home?"

"I was all set to leave," I admitted. "I thought I'd hit a dead end, and I was just wasting the Sanderses' money."

"And now?"

"Damn it, Lou, if they're still shooting at me, I'm close to something, even if I don't know what the hell it is."

"But was he shooting at you?" he asked. "I mean, did he know he was shooting at Eli Paxton? The way Bernice described it when she reported it to me, there's every possibility that he still doesn't know who he was shooting at this morning."

"That's probably true," I agreed.

"Then I don't follow you," said Berger.

"Jimenez is involved in this in some way. He tried to kill me a couple of nights ago. Today he may not have known it was me, but he was ready and willing to kill anyone who spotted him—and he had to know I was writing down his plate number or maybe taking a photo of him, something so that I slowed to a crawl right opposite him and then tried to hide my face." I finished the cigarette, reached for another, and exercised just enough willpower not to pull the pack out. "Now I have to assume he's not on the lam from the law anywhere, because he was willing to be seen during the auction. That means that whatever reason he had for shooting, it wasn't simply that someone in a green Chevy knew that this guy with no warrants out for his arrest was in Lexington."

He took a deep breath and released it slowly. "I hadn't thought of that," he admitted.

"Anyway," I concluded, "it's just vaguely possible that he recognized me, though he didn't get much of a look at me even the other night. It was dark, he ran me off the road, and then a couple of hours later he took a shot at me across a parking lot just half a second after I opened the door. He may not know even now what I look like. Maybe he does, but I'd give heavy odds that if you or Drew drove by him exactly the way I did, not in squad cars, he'd have shot at you too."

"Makes sense," he said. "But what the hell is there? I've pulled up a list of everyone who lives within a block of where you told Bernice he was parked. There are a few doctors, a lawyer, a minister, no breeders or trainers, no jockeys."

"If I knew that, I'd have this thing half solved," I said. "I'm still trying to find a connection between Tony and Billy. As far as anyone knows, they never met, not even once. One worked for Chessman and one worked for Standish. They didn't even have any friends in common, in or out of the horse business. The only link is that they rubbed the same horse, and one was gone before the other was hired."

"I wish I could say something useful," replied Berger. "You've pretty much convinced me they're dead, but there are no clues, no nothing. I'll help you all I can, and so will Drew, but I can't put a lot of men on this case. If one kid surfaces next month in Los Angeles and the other shows up a year from now in South Beach after we've spent a thousand man-hours trying to prove they've been killed, heads are going to roll around here, and I'm a little long in the tooth to retrain for a new profession."

"What about the Mercedes?" I asked.

"Rented in Tulsa," he said.

"To?"

Berger made a face. "Joe Smith."

"Well, at least you know you're looking for a Hispanic guy carrying a license that identifies him as Joe Smith," I said with a smile.

"We know who we're looking for," he said seriously.

Then one of his men stood in the doorway and cleared his throat.

"Yeah?" said Berger, turning to him.

"Seven-car pile-up on the interstate ramp, sir."

Berger turned to me. "Sorry. I've got to go figure out who's available to send to the scene of the idiocy."

I nodded, not that a show of disapproval would have kept him in the room, and then I was alone again and still puzzling over what the hell I was supposed to know that made me a target.

Things started getting busy—mostly traffic problems, but there was an attempted holdup at a currency exchange, a couple of domestic violence cases, and some kid stole some other kid's car. Lou was kept busy, Bernice was even busier, and Drew was still working the night shift, so I had the next couple of hours to amuse myself before Brenda showed up and Bernice and I could go out to dinner.

I figured what the hell, I hadn't shaved in a couple of days, so I might as well make use of the time. I went into the bathroom and got a good look at my face in the mirror. It needed a shave, all right; it probably also needed a couple of stitches, and it sure as hell needed a new ear lobe. I settled for just shaving around my lips—if I kissed her again, I didn't want her to come away looking as bloody as I looked this morning—and then I took a quick shower and changed into some un-blood-splattered clothes.

Then I sat down, hands behind my head, feet propped up on the cot, and spent another hour trying to figure out why the bad guys didn't care about me for a day or two after Tony vanished and Tyrone was sold and then wanted me dead. All I got for my efforts was a headache.

The time dragged by, and finally Bernice appeared in the doorway.

"Hungry?" she asked.

"For food, a bit," I answered her. "For company, more than you can imagine."

She smiled. "That's the nicest thing anyone's said to me all afternoon." Then: "What kind of food would you like?"

"Seriously?" I responded. "The kind where no one shoots at me."

"Not to worry," she said. "As long as I wear this uniform, I'm the primary target."

"Can I count on that?" I asked with a smile.

"Seriously, Eli, what kind of food would you like?"

"Right about now, I think I'd like anything that doesn't bite back."

She laughed. "All right. I know a nice secluded place . . ."

"Secluded is good," I interjected.

"It's about ten miles out of town and it's off by itself. No one sneaks up on this place."

"Sounds good to me."

"And I think we'd better take my car."

"Oh?" I said.

She smiled. "It's not a green Chevy."

"A telling point," I agreed.

There was no sense waiting for it to get dark; that doesn't happen until about 8:30 in Kentucky in June. So she sent a uniformed cop out to make sure no one was lurking nearby, and then we went to her car, a very comfortable Chrysler 200. She kept to less trafficked streets, just to make sure we weren't being followed, the city kind of petered out, and then we were out in farm country, but not quite horse country (no white plank fences), and a couple of minutes later she pulled up to what looked for all the world like a white brick farmhouse with a small parking area.

We entered, the waiter—who was probably the owner and possibly the chef as well—gave her a big hug and led us to a table, dropped off a couple of menus, and made himself scarce. There were twelve tables, and only five were occupied, including ours.

"Does this place do any business?" I asked.

"It's early, Eli. By the time we leave, every table will be filled, and there may even be a waiting line."

I began reading the menu—pure American top to bottom—and ordered a pure American meal of a rib eye steak and mashed potatoes.

"You come here often?" I asked while we were waiting for our food.

"Only when I'm hiding the good guys from the bad guys," she said. "I'm sorry; that wasn't funny. I come here about once a month. I've been doing it for years."

"Yeah, the whole staff—all one of him—seemed to know you."

"Oh, there's more than one," she replied, "but it's a family business. It used to be bigger. Jerry—that's the owner, the fellow who greeted us and took our order—had four kids helping him, but a daughter got married and moved out of state, and a son was killed in Afghanistan."

"Is he the cook?"

She shook her head. "His wife is."

We chatted a bit about everything except the events of the day, and then the food arrived and it was as good as she'd led me to believe it would be.

"Didn't you like it?" she asked when Jerry had cleared the table and brought us some coffee.

"It was fine," I said.

"You've got a sour face."

"It's not the food," I said.

"This afternoon," she said knowingly.

I shook my head. "No. I don't want to sound like Humphrey Bogart or Robert Mitchum, but sometimes that goes with the job. What's driving me crazy isn't that they're shooting at me for stumbling onto something. It's that I still don't know what the hell I've stumbled onto."

"I can understand your frustration," she said. "Would it help to talk about it?"

"I've been talking about it for three days, and everything keeps coming up blank," I said, unable to keep the frustration out of my voice. "If anything's happened to Tony, and that's still an unproven 'if,' there's no reason why it should have happened to Billy Paulson too. And of course I don't know if anything did happen to either of them. Then there's Bigelow. The man's clearly in deep financial trouble. If this was a movie, he'd be the perfect suspect. But first, how could killing either kid get him out of financial trouble? And second, I doubt that either kid spent five minutes total in his presence. They wouldn't have had any access to his records, there isn't a damned way they could hurt him, or blackmail him, or do anything that would make him want to get rid of them. As for the managers, Chessman never met Tony, and I don't think Standish ever met Billy." I took a swallow of my coffee, which was on the bitter side. "Okay," I concluded, "make sense out of that."

"I can't," she admitted. "If they're dead, the obvious question is: who benefits from their deaths? And if it's not Bigelow, or Standish, or Chessman, then maybe you're looking too close to home. Maybe there's some gambler who . . ." She stopped and shook her head. "No, that's wrong. Mill Creek doesn't race its horses, and neither does the farm Chessman went to. It can't have anything to do with gambling."

"You see my problem," I said with a smile.

"It's a hell of a problem," she agreed. "You solve this and I'll buy you a bottle of whatever you want, short of Dom Perignon. You'll have earned it."

"You're on a budget," I said. "I'll take an obscene dance instead."

"Solve it first, then we'll talk," she replied as Jerry brought two checks to the table. I grabbed them both before she could reach for hers.

"You paid for gas," I said.

She seemed about to protest, then just shrugged an acquiescence.

I left the money and tip on the table, and then we drove back to the station. She dropped me at the front door, stayed in the car—so much for shaving, I decided wryly—and drove off as I entered the building. Lou had gone home, but Drew MacDonald was there. He'd heard about what happened and asked me to fill him in, but he didn't have any more answers than Bernice did.

Finally I went to my room, closed the door, found that I wasn't sleepy—it was only eight-thirty—and sat down at the desk next to the pile of Tony's Thoroughbred Weekly magazines and the box with Billy Paulson's stuff. I picked up Eddie Arcaro's whip and tried to imagine what it felt like to be riding Citation or Whirlaway home ten lengths in front of the field. Probably the way Dick Tracy felt whenever he put a super-villain behind bars. It was a feeling I could only imagine.

I finally put the whip back in the box and pulled out the inscribed photo again. I didn't know that much about horses, but I could tell that Tyrone was a handsome-looking animal, even with that scar on his neck. Since Billy was holding the rope that was attached to his halter, Tyrone figured to be under a year old in the shot, and he was already exuding class and power. I replaced the photo in its envelope, pushed the box aside, and opened a Thoroughbred Weekly from March. A photo of the finish of the Flamingo Stakes was on the cover—three noses on the wire, I read about it being the race of the year so far, and I began idly thumbing through the pages. After a couple of minutes I put it aside and picked up the most recent issue, from two weeks ago. It was much thicker than the March issue, which figured, because there must have been fifty pages of ads for yearlings that would be auctioned at Keeneland. I thumbed through it, looking for Tyrone, and I found him in an ad for the Mill Creek yearlings. He had a full page to himself, as befitted the first Trojan colt ever to be sold at auction, and I spotted him by the scar even before I saw his pedigree with his parents in incredibly bold letters.

I stared at the photo for a moment and thought, And I actually petted you. Somehow I knew that was as close to that kind of quality as I was ever going to get.

I finally put the issue aside and picked one up from February, which covered the San Antonio Handicap and some other big-money races. I began thumbing through the various issues, and suddenly one of the December issues from the previous winter caught my eye. It boasted an article about the first crops of Trojan and the imported British champion Morpheus.

I opened it and soon came to a photo spread showing every Trojan and Morpheus colt and filly that was scheduled to be sold at auction during the coming year. To my untrained eye they were all good-looking horses. The Morpheus offspring were mostly blacks and dark bays, the Trojans mostly chestnuts with the occasional bay or gray thrown in for good measure. I spotted Tyrone and his scar right away. The pose looked very familiar, and I realized it was the same photo that Chessman had sent to Billy—but with Billy, who was standing at the edge of it, cut out.

Or was it the same? Maybe his feet were placed differently. Not that it mattered, but just out of curiosity I pulled Billy's photo out of the box and took another look.

And suddenly I knew what question I had failed to ask, and I even knew where I had to go for the answer.

27.

When morning came I was up almost with the sun and waited impatiently for a couple of hours until I was pretty sure my destination would be open for business. I had one of the officers take the Chevy back and get me a Toyota Camry that was a nice, nondescript gray. Then I packed what I needed in a large manila envelope and headed for the door. Bernice was just showing up for work as I was leaving.

"You look happy today," she remarked.

"It must be the sight of a pretty woman so early in the day," I said, giving her a peck on the cheek.

"You've figured something out," she said instantly.

"Yes, I have," I replied.

"Well?"

"Well what?"

"Are you going to tell me about it or not?" she demanded.

"I'm just checking it out, and then I'll be happy to tell anyone who'll listen," I said.

She stared at me. "So go already," she said. "We've all been going a little crazy trying to figure out what's happening. I hope whatever you've got holds up."

"That's what I'm off to find out."

"Good luck, Eli," she said as I walked out the door. "I mean it."

"I know you do."

The Camry felt a little cramped, but I wasn't going on a long trip. It had a GPS, but I had no idea how it worked. I laid the street map out on the passenger's seat so that I could refer to it if I needed to, and took off.

A few minutes later I pulled into a small lot and realized I was only

165

a couple of blocks from the Hyatt where I'd met Ben Miller for what had seemed like an uneventful few days of standing guard over a horse.

I climbed a few steps to the entrance of the building I wanted, opened the door, and found myself standing in front of a pretty blonde at a reception desk.

"Welcome to the Thoroughbred Weekly," she greeted me. "How may I help you?"

I flashed my detective's license. "I'd like to speak to whoever's in charge of the magazine—and tell him that I'm just seeking some information for a case I'm working on, nothing more."

"That would be Mr. Kent, our editor," she said. "Just a moment, please."

She picked up her phone, punched out three numbers, and spoke very softly into it. She hung up a few seconds later. "He's in conference right now," she said. "It should take about ten more minutes. Won't you please wait in our lobby? There's coffee on the counter there."

I thanked her and walked to the lobby, which was filled with leather furniture I wished I could take home with me. I poured myself a cup of coffee, added cream and sweetener, and saw that there was a complimentary stack of the current issue. I picked one up and looked at it. Tyrone was on the cover, standing in the sales ring, while the caption explained that he was the sales topper by half a million dollars.

I sat down, sipping my coffee and thumbing through the magazine. I found I was getting to know a number of the farms and stallions from their ads, as well as some of the current stakes winners, at least the ones who kept repeating their victories.

I was just reading an article about how the field for the Hollywood Gold Cup was shaping up when the blonde walked over and told me that Mr. Kent would see me now.

I got up and followed her as she led the way past a maze of work stations until we came to an office at the back of the building. She opened the door, walked inside, and waited for me to join her.

"This is Officer Paxton, sir," she said.

A handsome man in his late forties or early fifties with a head of wavy gray hair stood up. "Thanks, Linda," he said in a voice that had the faintest trace of a Southern accent. "I'll take it from here."

She nodded and left without a word, closing the door behind her.

"Have a seat, Lieutenant," he said, indicating a comfortable chair opposite his desk. "Or is it Captain?"

I smiled and shook my head. "Neither," I replied. "I'm not a cop; I'm a private detective. I can show you my license if you'd like."

"I don't think that'll be necessary, as long as we're not being arrested."

"You're not," I assured him.

"All right, Mr. Paxton."

"Eli," I said.

"All right, Eli. And I'm Jason. What can I do for you?"

I pulled the photo Chessman had sent to Billy Paulson of himself and Tyrone out of the envelope and laid it on his desk. "Do you recognize this picture?"

He studied it for a moment, then looked up, frowning. "Should I?"

"That's what I'm asking you."

"I don't want to sound careless or uninterested, Eli," he said, "but we get hundreds of photos in every week. Between races and ads, we probably run close to eighty, maybe even more in the summer, in each issue of the magazine."

"Take a good look," I said. "Take as long as you need."

He stared at it intently. "It looks like the sales topper, that Trojan colt, but I don't know if I've seen this particular photo before. I don't recognize the young man who's holding him."

"The groom's name is Billy Paulson," I said, making very sure not to say that it was Billy Paulson, in the past tense. "Let me ask you one more question about it. Why do you think it's the Trojan colt?"

"Right conformation, right color, and the scar is a dead giveaway."

"I agree," I said.

He looked puzzled. "And that's it?"

"Not quite," I said. I pulled the December issue out of the envelope, opened it to the page I'd marked by folding its upper corner, and pushed it across the desk to him. "How about this one?"

"Same colt," he said instantly.

"You're sure?"

He nodded his head. "Hell, I think it's even the same photo, except that the groom's been cut out."

"I think it's the same photo, too," I said. "Would you have a copy of the photo on file here?"

"Certainly. If not the actual photo, than a high-resolution scan of it. We keep every photo that comes in here." A quick smile. "Thanks to computers, what used to fill four storage rooms now fits in one tower and a couple of externals."

"And you don't see anything peculiar about the photo you ran?"

He looked again and shook his head. "Not a bit," he said easily. "Look, Eli, if a world-famous trainer like Todd Pletcher or Bob Baffert was at the other end of the rope, of course we'd have left him in, but no one wants to see a kid who just rubs down the horse."

I shook my head impatiently. "That's not what I'm talking about. Look again."

Kent looked and shrugged. "Same picture, absolutely."

"But in the magazine the scar's on the right side of his neck, and in the original it's on the left side," I half-yelled.

"Is that what this is all about?" he asked with a smile.

"Absolutely."

"I can see that an explanation is in order," he said.

I nodded my head. "It sure as hell is," I said. "I want to know why you reversed the photo."

He frowned. "Reversed?" he repeated, and then seemed to relax again. "Let me initiate you into the terminology of the publishing business, Eli. Reverse would be to change something that was white on black to something that was black on white. What we did with this photo was to flop it. That's the term: to flop an image. Right becomes left, left becomes right."

"You make it sound like it's a standard practice," I said.

"It is."

"Why?" I asked. "I mean, no disrespect, but a horse is a horse. Who cares which way he's facing?"

"Mr. Geller—he's our publisher—cares," answered Kent. "It's our policy—well, his policy, which makes it our policy—that whenever possible the horse should be looking off the page, to the open spaces, which he's theoretically going to run through any second. So if he's on a left-hand page, he faces left, and if he's on a right-hand page, he faces right. We try not to have him facing the middle of the magazine; no wide open spaces there."

I thumbed through the magazine, and in another three pages I found a horse on a left-hand page racing hell for leather toward the center of the magazine.

"Then explain this, please," I said, trying to keep the frustration out of my voice.

He looked at it and smiled.

"What do you see, Eli?"

"Same as you," I said. "I see a horse and jockey crossing the finish line and heading right for the middle of the magazine."

"You see a filly with the number '4' on her saddlecloth winning the Santa Ynez Stakes at Santa Anita. We try to have them all look off into the distance beyond the magazine, but we run dozens of photos of races, and it would look damned silly to flop the photo if it meant we flopped the saddlecloth number and the figures on the tote board in the infield. Even Mr. Geller understands there are limitations to flopping photos."

I thought about what he said. I was about to apologize for taking up his time and was preparing to go back to square one of the whole damned problem, when something else occurred to me.

"You say you have the original photo, a duplicate of this one"—I indicated Billy's photo—"on file here?"

"Yes."

"Probably on your computer?"

"Definitely on our computer."

"Would it be flopped?" I asked.

He shook his head. "No, it would be preserved exactly the way it came in. If this colt goes out and wins the Derby or the Breeders' Cup, we may do a retrospective of him, but we can't know now whether he'll be on an odd-numbered or even-numbered page."

"I see," I said. "I have one last favor to ask. Can you pull up the original and make absolutely sure it was the same as the one I brought in, that indeed you flopped it?"

"I can tell you right now that it'll be the same," he said, and I caught a little annoyance creeping into his voice. "I don't know what grand conspiracy you were imagining, but I assure you again that there is absolutely nothing unusual about flopping a photo of a horse, a dog, a Playmate, anything where the flopping doesn't make the viewer do a double-take, such as when letters or numbers are included."

"I know, and I believe you," I said. "But if I can just see it, I'll be out of your hair forever."

He grimaced and sighed. "All right. It'll take a couple of minutes."

He reached for the issue, got the date from the cover, picked up his phone, and punched in some numbers.

"Hello, Bill?" he said. "This is Jason. In the December 23rd issue we ran a spread of photos on potential auction yearlings from the first crops of Trojan and Morpheus. Print out the photo of Bigelow's Trojan colt, the one who just topped the sale, and bring it in, would you, please? Yes, right away, thanks."

He hung up the phone and looked at me, not without a degree of pity.

"I'm sorry to destroy your big case for you," he said. "You saw the flopped photo and thought someone ran a ringer through the sales ring." He shook his head. "Too bad. It would have made a helluva story."

A minute later a young black man entered the office with a sheet of paper and laid it on Kent's desk.

"Thanks, Bill," said Kent.

"Anything else?" asked Bill.

"No, that'll be it."

The young man left the office. Kent looked at the printout of the photo and passed it across the desk to me.

"Same photo," he said. "Facing the same way as your photo, with the same kid holding him in the same pose. Satisfied?"

I gave him a huge grin. "More than satisfied," I said. "Elated."

He looked puzzled. "I don't follow you, Eli," he said. "What do you think you know that I don't know?"

I kept grinning. "Tell me again why there are some photos you can't flop."

"Like I said, if they've got letters or numbers, they come out backward."

I tossed the current issue of Thoroughbred Weekly onto his desk. "Tell me what you see."

"The Trojan colt. Scar's on the right side, so we probably flopped it again. There are less people off to the right, so we had him look that way."

"You didn't flop it," I told him.

"What makes you think not?"

I pointed to the "213" on his hip.

"If the scar is on his left side, those numbers would be flopped too—and they're not," I said. "You ever hear of a scar migrating from one side of a horse's neck to another?"

He picked up the magazine and held it side-by-side with the photo.

"Well, I'll be damned!" he muttered.

28.

Kent was silent for a long minute as the revelation sank in. Finally he came back to life.

"My God, Eli, what a story you've uncovered! Even before we print it, I've got to talk to the TOBA—that's the Thoroughbred Owners and Breeders Association—and tell them what's happened! Oh, and Fasig-Tipton! They've got to know too!"

"They'll all know," I assured him. "But not yet."

He stared at me. "I can't keep something like this quiet. I mean, you're talking about a three-million-dollar scam!"

"That's just the tip of the iceberg," I said.

He frowned. "What the hell are you talking about?" he demanded.

"There is almost certainly a murder connected with this, and probably two," I explained. "You've got to keep this quiet until I can piece together the evidence I need to nail the killer."

"Eli, this is more than my profession," said Kent. "The racing industry is my life. I can't stand by quietly now that I'm aware of what may be the biggest single fraud ever perpetrated on it! They have to be informed, to be warned!"

"It should just be for a few more days," I said. "But if word gets out that we know what happened, the people I'm after are going to start running. And off the record, they've already started shooting."

His face reflected his indecision. "I don't know . . ." he began.

I could sympathize with him. He wasn't looking to beat his competition for a Pulitzer Prize. He was concerned with the integrity of the industry he loved and to which he'd devoted his life.

"All right," I said. "I gave you the story of the decade. Now I want you to do me a favor."

"What?" he asked suspiciously.

"Come for a ten-minute ride with me."

"Where?"

"I'm cooperating with the cops at a local police station. You know nothing about me, and you probably distrust my motives, or maybe you think I'm out for some personal glory, and I'm probably not going to convince you otherwise by myself. But if the Lexington police explain why this has to be kept secret for a few more days, that we are after more than a crooked consignor, and that we'll give you all the details first when we break the case, will you listen to them?"

He stared at me for a minute, then got to his feet. "Let's go."

He stopped by the reception desk to explain that he'd be gone for an hour, and then we went out to the parking lot. I led him to the Camry. He took one look and walked over to a silver Lincoln.

"Let's use this one," he suggested.

I had no problem with that, and a moment later we were on our way to "my" police station, passing two others along the way. He tried to start a conversation about the upcoming weekend races, and when that didn't work, about which European horses figured to ship here for the Breeders' Cup races in the fall, and when that didn't work either, he began diagnosing the strengths and weaknesses of the Kentucky Wild-cats'—excuse me: Big Blue's—basketball team. I began to get the distinct impression that he lived, breathed, ate, and slept horse racing and beyond that was interested in very little else.

We pulled into the police station and got out of the car. We entered the building and were greeted by Bernice.

"Hi, Eli," she said.

"Bernice, this is Jason Kent, the editor of the Thoroughbred Weekly. Is Lou in?"

"Yes."

"And alone?"

"I think so, yes."

"We'd like to see him."

"You know the way," she said.

"You've been involved in this too," I said. "I'd be happy to have you in there."

"You go ahead," she said. "I'll be along in a minute or two, as soon as I get someone to watch the desk here."

"Thanks," I said as Kent and I headed down the corridor to Lou Berger's office. Berger was reading reports on his computer screen as we entered. He stood up and turned to face us.

"Hi, Lou," I said. "This gentleman is Jason Kent, the editor of—"

"I know who he is," said Berger. "You look younger than your picture," he continued, extending his hand.

"Which picture is that?" asked Kent, taking and shaking Berger's hand.

"The Thoroughbred Breeders dinner a couple of weeks back. You were handing out some award."

"Yeah, that was me," said Kent. "And as I recall, I'd just flown in from England where I'd gone for the Epsom Derby. I hadn't slept in forty-eight hours."

"Have a seat, Mr. Kent," said Berger.

"Jason," said Kent, sitting down.

"You too, Eli," continued Berger, turning to me. "And you'd better tell me what this is all about. You look so excited I'd guess you were either about to offer up a major revelation or wet your pants."

"Sounds like I got here just in time," said Bernice from the doorway. "Shame I didn't bring my camera."

"Well?" persisted Berger.

"Lou," I said, "the Trojan colt was a ringer!"

He looked dubious, and as she walked into my line of vision, so did Bernice. Things like that just didn't happen at the Select Sales.

I explained that I'd seen the original photo—as they had—in Billy Paulson's possessions, and that when it didn't match the scar in the magazine's photos I went down to the Thoroughbred Weekly's office and asked Kent about it. He told me about the practice of flopping photos, which explained everything up to the photo of Tyrone in the ring with his hip number clearly not flopped.

"Sonuvabitch!" said Berger. "Well, now we know how Bigelow planned to get out of debt." Suddenly he frowned. "But why a ringer? Surely he can't sell the real Trojan colt now. If this one is supposed to be the Trojan colt, then what can he get for the real one, sticking this one's pedigree on it—fifty thousand? A hundred, tops?"

"I agree," I said.

"So do I," chimed in Kent. "He sold his best-bred stock at the sale. Any yearlings he has left aren't worth that much."

Bernice had a sly smile on her face. "Do you want to tell them, Eli, or should I?"

I returned the smile. "You doped it out?" I said. "Be my guest."

"There's only one reason he'd risk everything by selling a ringer," she said. "The real Trojan colt is dead—and he needed that purchase price to avoid going under."

"And whoever matched the scar on the ringer used the photo in the December issue of Thoroughbred Weekly," I added. "A photo that showed the scar on the right side of the neck."

"Goddamn!" said Berger. "That makes sense!"

"You know, it does at that," agreed Kent. Then he frowned. "I hope no one will think my magazine's in collusion on this."

"How could they?" said Bernice. "The Trojan colt was alive when you ran the photo."

"Oh, yes, of course," said Kent, sounding much relieved.

"What I don't know is how they even got the ringer into the sale," I said. "Doesn't his implanted chip give him away?"

Kent frowned. "What implanted chip?"

"I think all domestic animals have them," I said. "I've got a dog that can't be worth five dollars on the open market, and he has one."

Kent shook his head. "Thoroughbreds are different. They're identified by a lip tattoo, and the Jockey Club doesn't require the tattoo until the first time the horse goes to the post. Most get them sooner, but it's not a requirement."

"Well," I said with a shrug, "that's how they got away with it. The Jockey Club may remain in the dark, but we're not the first to figure out what happened. Billy Paulson and Tony Sanders were his grooms, and they're both missing. I'd be surprised if they hadn't doped it out, and I'd be even more surprised if either of them is still alive."

"So you really think a murder was committed?" asked Kent.

"More than one," I said. "The two of them didn't know each other, never met, and disappeared more than a month apart."

"Jesus!" whispered Kent hoarsely.

"We couldn't make any progress until this morning, until I knew why someone would want to get rid of them," I explained to him. "But now that we know, we can start putting the pieces together. Only one thing can stop us."

He stared at me. "Me?" he said.

"Releasing what we just discussed before we're ready to move," confirmed Berger, who clearly had figured out why I'd brought Kent along to the office. "We're pretty sure Bigelow's behind it. After all, he's the only one who had anything to lose with the death of the colt. And we think we know who pulled the trigger . . ."

"They've been shot?" exclaimed Kent. "But I thought they were both missing!"

"A figure of speech," said Berger. "We've got a suspect in Bigelow, and we think we know how he got the job done. We've identified a possible hit man. What we need now are some details, not many, just enough to justify arresting them and not have a lawyer spring them the same afternoon . . ."

"Them?" repeated Kent. "I'm confused again."

"I don't want to use names until we're sure," said Berger. "Let's say Bigelow and his coconspirator."

"All right," said Kent, nodding his head. "I can see that."

"We're close," continued Berger. "Very close. I'd hate to blow it now. Can we count on you to keep this a secret until we resolve it?"

"There's got to be a time limit," said Kent. "Eli's from out of town, but you two live here. You know how much this area depends on the thoroughbred industry, and how much an industry that's basically supported by gambling depends on its integrity. A serious fraud has been committed here, and we've got to end it as quickly as possible, or you could see an awful lot of damage done to an industry that we all depend on." He paused while we considered his words. "That's for the industry. As for the magazine, we'll put it off for as long as necessary, provided that Eli keeps his word."

"His word?" asked Berger.

"He gives us all the details and gives Thoroughbred Weekly first shot at it."

"That might be difficult, if we march Bigelow out of his mansion in handcuffs," said Bernice.

"How's this?" I suggested. "We'll give your magazine all the details of the ringer story with a one-week head start on your competition. I think you have to agree that we can't keep everything a secret if we arrest a prominent citizen for murder."

"We'll also credit you and Thoroughbred Weekly for helping crack the case," added Berger.

Kent considered it for a moment, then nodded his agreement.

"I agree, of course," he said. "I'm not going to be responsible for letting that bastard get away with fraud in our most prestigious sale."

"Fraud and murder," said Bernice.

Kent shrugged. "And murder," he agreed. It seemed like an afterthought.

"All right," said Berger, getting to his feet, and Kent and I followed suit. "We have an agreement."

They shook hands. Bernice went back to her desk, and Kent and I headed out of the office.

"I want you back here as soon as possible, Eli," said Berger. "We've got a killer to catch."

"Catching him should be easy," I said. "We know where he lives. Proving he's a killer is another matter."

He sighed heavily. "Yeah," he replied. "I know."

29.

I was back in Berger's office half an hour later. He'd called MacDonald in on what I guessed was two hours' sleep, and Bernice was there too.

I walked in and sat down.

"Morning," croaked MacDonald.

"Bernice, close the door," said Berger, and she walked over and did so. "All right," he said. "I've filled Drew in on the ringer. If I were a betting man, I'd say it's even money that both kids were murdered, and a dead certainty that the Sanders kid was. So the first question is: how are they connected?"

"Except for both being killed by Bigelow, or rather having their deaths commissioned by Bigelow, I don't see how they can be," I said. "Remember, the two never met, and if they were killed—and I think they were—they were killed more than a month apart."

"And we do know Jimenez was in town when each kid turned up missing," added MacDonald.

"Have they ever worked together before, I wonder?" mused Berger.

"The kids?" said Bernice. "They never even met."

"No, I mean Bigelow and Jimenez," replied Berger.

"If they have, we sure as hell wouldn't know about it," said Mac-Donald. "After all, Jimenez is still on the loose, and no one's accused Bigelow of anything like murder in the past."

"Okay," said Berger. "Has anyone got any theories?"

"I don't think you have to be a genius to dope out the Paulson end of it," said Bernice. "After, he worked for Bigelow last year. He handled the real Trojan colt, so he had to know there'd been a switch."

"Right," I said. "If he was looking for some easy money—big money—he'd have played along and let Bigelow give him a few hundred dollars here and there while keeping the secret until he figured out what the colt was worth. But once the colt was approved for the Select Sale and people started talking about what he might bring, the kid probably confronted Bigelow and demanded some really big money to keep his mouth shut."

"Why just Paulson?" asked Berger. "What about the rest of the staff?"

"He was just about the only holdover when Standish got here," I said, "and probably the only one who knew what had happened. In fact, he had to know. He was in charge of the original, so whatever happened to it—broken leg, colic, anything—he'd have been right on the scene. He knew what was going on, all right, and clearly he was paid to keep quiet. Then he got greedy and went from being a conspirator to a blackmailer."

"So the way you figure it, he waited until Keeneland accepted the ringer, then went to Bigelow and threatened to expose him?"

"Right," I said. "That's the only way it figures. Why else would he keep his mouth shut? And once the blackmail started, I figure Bigelow maybe paid him one small chunk and promised to pay him every week or told him it would take a few days to get the kind of cash the kid was talking about, and then he sent for Jimenez, so even if the body turned up full of bullet holes, you'd probably be looking for a local hitter."

"Okay, that makes sense," said Berger.

"Just one problem," added MacDonald. "It sounds good, it makes sense, it feels right—but without a body it's all just theory."

"And they've had plenty of time to hide the body," said Berger.

"I agree," said Bernice. "I think we should be concentrating on the Sanders boy. Eli knew him, he's only been gone a few days, and that trail has to be fresher."

"Right," I said. "If I just knew one thing, we could probably break this open in two minutes."

"What thing?"

"The same thing that's been driving me crazy since I came across it," I answered. "What the hell was Tony doing near the Leestown Road Kroger the night he went missing? Whatever he was doing there, he had to figure he'd be fifteen minutes tops, because it was due to rain again in another half hour or so, and he left the top down on his convertible."

"And that's also where Jimenez shot at you," added Bernice.

"The second time," I said. "The first was at my motel."

"I wish I knew what to do next," said Berger. "We could bring Bigelow in and sweat him, but he's bound to come equipped with a team of high-powered lawyers. They won't let him give anything but his name, rank, and serial number, and there's no way we can keep him locked up overnight, so all we'd accomplish would be to let him know what we know."

"I agree," said MacDonald. "We don't touch him until we have something concrete."

They all turned to me.

"I'll go back to Mill Creek and look around again." I grimaced. "I just wish I knew what I was looking for."

"You might talk to the other guy, too," said Berger. "The one who used to work there."

"You mean Hal Chessman?" I asked. "He never laid eyes on Tony. He's been gone since Christmas."

Berger grimaced. "I know, I know. I'm clutching at straws. You know the kids were killed, I know it, Drew and Bernice know it. But along with lacking a shred of proof, we've got a guy who thinks the greatest crime committed, whether they were killed or not, was that someone sold a ringer for three million bucks, and I saw a fanatical glow in his eyes. I don't know if Jason Kent can keep his mouth shut for more than a week."

"Well, at least we've got that much on Bigelow," said MacDonald. "If we can't prove a murder, we can nail him on selling the ringer."

"I don't give a damn about that," I said harshly.

They all looked at me.

"I'm not a cop. I've been paid to find Tony Sanders, or to find out what happened to him, and putting one more slimeball in jail for fraud isn't going to help my clients."

"Well, there's got to be a time limit, Eli," said Berger. "I'd give you a month or two, but there's a major sale at Saratoga next month, and even if Bigelow hasn't got anything in that one, he'll be selling his lesser-bred yearlings this fall at Keeneland, and you know Jason Kent's not going to wait anywhere near that long."

I sighed deeply. "I know."

"Okay, go back to the farm, talk to the trainer, talk to the staff, talk to Bigelow if you think it'll help, do what you can. There's got to be some proof somewhere."

I nodded my head. "I agree. It's just a matter of finding it. And," I added, "there is one more thing to consider."

"What's that?"

"Maybe whatever happened to the real Trojan colt happened so fast there was never any chance of saving him. Maybe he broke a leg, and five minutes later Bigelow or Paulson put a bullet in his brain. But there's one thing neither of them had the skill to do."

"Yeah?" said Berger.

"Duplicate that scar. Screw it up and you've got a festering wound on a three-million-dollar yearling, and if it heals wrong, it won't look like the scar in the flopped photo. So while I'm looking around the farm again, you might see if any veterinarians have been reported missing anytime since the end of December, when Chessman left the farm and before Standish arrived."

"That's not a bad idea," said Berger.

"It's a damned good one," Bernice chimed in.

"Anything else?" said Berger.

I checked my watch. "I'll grab a quick lunch and pop back out to the farm."

"I'll go with you," said MacDonald. "I'm going to eat and then grab a couple more hours' sleep before I come back to work for the night."

"Tilly's?" I asked.

"Of course."

We drove there in his car. He just had coffee and a slice of pie. I had a hot brown, a kind of sandwich that's unique to Kentucky, though it's on the menu in two or three restaurants in Cincinnati.

Then he dropped me at the station, I got into the Camry, and drove out to Mill Creek to make one last attempt to find out what happened to a troubled young man named Tony Sanders.

30.

I drove up the long driveway with the mansion on the right and the barns and paddocks on the left, turned and parked at the biggest barn, and got out of the Camry. Jeremy came out of the barn and greeted me.

"Back again, Mr. Paxton?" he said.

"Yeah," I replied. "Is Frank around?"

"He's in his office," he said, indicating the barn. "Any word about Tony yet?"

"I'm still working on it."

"Too bad. He was a nice kid. I hope he's having a good time on whatever beach he wound up on."

"I hope so too," I said, walking past him and entering the barn. I went directly to Standish's office and stood in the doorway for a moment until he looked up.

"We're going to have to start charging you board," he said with a smile.

"Just making what I hope is my last tour of the place."

"You've got some leads?"

I shook my head. "Nope. Just looking around again."

"Looking for . . . ?"

"Damned if I know," I said. "Same as the last few times: anything that'll tell me where Tony Sanders might be."

"So you haven't made any progress?" said Standish. "I hope he's okay. He was a good kid. I hate to think of him lying outside somewhere with maybe a busted ankle."

"I sure as hell doubt that's the case," I said. "He could have crawled to Louisville by now."

"True," agreed Standish. "I really don't know why he left. He liked the work, he loved the business, and everyone here liked him. Hell, even Mr. Bigelow liked him."

"Oh?" I said, raising an eyebrow. "I thought he barely knew him."

"Maybe I worded that wrong," replied Standish with a smile. "What I meant is that he appreciated the job that Tony did with Tyrone. He had the colt in perfect shape for the sale, and you know how valuable that turned out to be." He paused. "In fact, just a few hours after Tyrone sold, Bigelow declared it Tony Sanders Night."

"He did?" I asked curiously.

Standish nodded. "He gave me a couple of hundred dollars and had me take the night staff—there are six of them—to the movies in the farm's van, and then to a late-night dinner. Of course, the guest of honor was missing . . . but still, it was a nice gesture, and they had a great time. One of the half-price rerun houses was showing a pair of the old Sean Connery James Bond films. I hadn't seen them, even on television, in maybe fifteen years."

"Sounds like fun," I remarked.

"It was. I know Bigelow's having a lot of financial troubles, so that made it even more generous of him."

"I can't argue that."

He got to his feet. "Come on," he said. "I've got something to show you."

He walked out of the office and down the aisle until he was outside, with me just a step behind him. We began walking between the paddocks and finally came to one that housed four mares—two bays, a gray, and a chestnut—and their offspring, which looked like they ranged from two to maybe four months old.

"Okay," I said. "What am I looking at?"

"See the chestnut mare?"

"Yeah."

"That's Tyrone's mother. And the little chestnut filly running around is his half sister, by Instant Replay." He paused and turned to me. "If you find Tony, tell him I don't care why he went AWOL, his job is still waiting for him, and I'm saving the filly for him."

"I'll do that," I said.

"We had quite a fight to keep her alive," Standish continued. "It was a rough birth."

"Especially without a vet on the grounds," I said. "Who do you use?"

"Jim Grady," he answered. "I brought him with me. Which is to say, I convinced Bigelow to use him when I came to work here. He's about six miles away, but he'll come out any time of the night or day on a moment's notice. I've been using him for, oh, it must be fifteen years now."

We watched the foals frisking about for a few minutes, then turned and headed back to the big barn.

"Got a question," I said as we walked. "I know Tony's job at Keeneland was to stick with Tyrone around the clock, but surely he had other duties on the farm here?"

Standish nodded his head. "He had four other yearlings as well, including a filly who sold the night after Tyrone, he helped with some of the babies, and while he wasn't a foaling man, he'd spend about every fifth or sixth night here, keeping an eye on mares who were about to drop their foals. He knew which staff members to call, and if there were problems after that, it was out of his hands. Once the foaling team showed up, he was free to leave."

"So he walked the foals into the barns at night or when it was raining or snowing?" I asked.

He chuckled. "He walked the *mares* in and the foals followed on their own. Try to lead a month-old or two-month-old foal away from its mother and you've got a panicky foal, and half the time a panicky thousand-pound mare as well."

"Which barns would he have put them in?" I asked. "I just need to take one look to make sure I'm not missing anything."

He pointed out three barns to me, left me to my own devices, and walked back to his office. I waved to a couple of grooms I recognized, entered each barn in turn, examined the tack rooms and any other areas I could think to look, and found absolutely nothing relating to Tony in any way.

It was frustrating. I had the run of the farm, carte blanche to peek into every corner. I *knew* Billy Paulson was dead, and I'd have given long odds that Tony had been killed too, but I couldn't pick up a single piece of evidence, couldn't add a thing to what I'd found—or failed to find—the last few times I'd come to the farm. Standish had been absolutely open with me, hadn't made a single corner of the multitude of barns or hundreds of acres off-limits to me, and still I kept coming up blank.

Somehow I knew I wouldn't be back looking for clues or leads again. You only get so many strikes in a baseball game or an investigation before you become a failure and then a nuisance.

All right, I thought as I walked to the car, *there's nothing to be learned here*. It was useless to talk to Jason Kent; he didn't know a damned thing until I'd visited him in his office this morning. There was no sense confronting Bigelow; comic books and bad movies to the contrary, mighty few criminals brag about all the details of their crimes to the good guys.

I went through the whole cast of characters in my mind. There was only one left to speak to, the least likely of all to help me track down Tony Sanders. But I had simply run out of alternatives, so I started the Camry and headed off to Blue Banner Farm to talk to Hal Chessman.

31.

Chessman was in Blue Banner's breeding barn when one of the hired help told him I was there. He came out a minute later to greet me.

"Hi, Eli," he said with a welcoming smile on his pudgy face. "We're just introducing Marauder to one of today's lady friends. Care to watch?"

"I think I'll take a pass," I said. "If he can score on the first date, it'll just depress me."

He laughed at that. "So what can I do for you?"

A stallion's shrill, impatient scream came from the barn.

"Take care of *his* needs first," I said. "Mine can wait a few minutes."

"It won't be long," he said. "I'm really just overseeing the men who are actually working with the horses."

He disappeared into the barn as Marauder screamed again, and I heard an answering scream coming from deeper in the stallion barn, a scream that sounded very jealous to me. They had a bunch of stallions at the farm, but somehow I was sure it came from Pit Boss, who'd always been a fierce competitor on the track.

There was some more noise, and then Chessman's voice barking orders, and then silence, and ten minutes later he emerged from the barn again.

"Everyone needs a rest," he announced. "That's the fifth mare today—and the second one for Marauder. I'm giving them all an hour off before the next one."

"Is there someplace where we can talk in private?" I asked.

"Tell you what," he said. "I've been up since six-thirty, and it's getting near my dinnertime. Why don't you join me—my treat—and we'll talk there?"

"Sounds good to me," I said. "At least let me do the driving."

"It's a deal," he said. He stopped a passing employee, told him that he'd be back in an hour or so, and then we walked to my car.

"This is a special place we're going to," he said as he started giving me directions.

"Let me guess," I said. "Tilly's?"

He laughed. "Funny," he said. "You don't look like a native."

"I've been in the company of some," I answered.

We got there in about seven or eight minutes and took a booth in the back. Neither of us looked at a menu. Chessman ordered some salt-cured ham, and I'd liked the hot brown so much I ordered it again. We each ordered a beer.

"Okay," he said when Tilly had delivered our beers and gone back behind the counter. "How's the search coming?"

"It's expanded beyond the Sanders kid," I said.

"Oh?"

"I want it understood that what I'm telling you is in confidence and goes no farther until I okay it."

He frowned. "You've got it."

"Let me start with a question," I said. "Were you at the sale?"

He shook his head. "Blue Banner Farm supports the Saratoga Sale. We didn't have any yearlings up at Keeneland, so I didn't see any reason to go. Besides, yearlings are another union at Blue Banner; I'm the stallion manager."

"One more question," I said. "When is the last time you saw the sales topper?"

"You mean Tyrone?" he said. "Probably about Christmas, give or take a few days. Why?"

"That was a ringer they sold at Keeneland," I told him.

"What are you talking about?" he demanded in loud tones, and a couple of diners turned to stare at us. "

"Lower your voice," I said. "This isn't for public consumption."

"Sorry," he said. "Now tell me about this."

"Something happened to the real Trojan colt between when you left Mill Creek and Frank Standish arrived," I said. "It's almost certain that he died in the interim."

"But that's crazy!" said Chessman.

"It's true," I insisted.

"What makes you think so?"

I told him how I'd doped it out. He interrupted once to explain about how flopping photos was a common practice at the magazine. When I told him the kicker, that the hip numbers weren't flopped and that meant the cover photo wasn't flopped, he had to agree.

"I'll be damned!" he said. "It's no secret that Travis is hurting for money. His one way out was that colt, and then it breaks something or dies from colic. He's in a blind panic, and then it occurs to him: he's got a look-alike chestnut colt, no white markings anywhere, same as Tyrone, and he figures: why not substitute it? I've already gone, almost all my staff has come away with me, and Frank Standish hasn't arrived yet. Probably the only guy who knows is Billy." Suddenly he stopped and blinked his eyes very rapidly for a few seconds. "Oh, shit! Billy had to be in on it, didn't he?"

I nodded my agreement. "He couldn't have pulled it off if Billy wasn't a coconspirator."

"Billy didn't run away," said Chessman firmly. "That bastard killed him."

"That's the way it figures," I agreed.

"So is your kid dead too?"

"You mean Tony Sanders?" I asked. "Yeah, I think so."

"These kids get so greedy today..." His voice trailed off and he shook his head sadly.

"I don't think Tony was in on it," I said.

"Oh?"

"I spent a few days with him during the sale," I said. "The kid was happy, carefree, lived for the sport. Then I go out for dinner the night before the ringer's sold, I'm gone half an hour, forty minutes tops, I come back, and suddenly Tony's got the weight of the world on his shoulders. He's worried as hell, anyone can see that. He knows I'm a detective, and he says he wants to tell me about it."

"So did he?"

I shook my head. "He said he had to talk to someone first, and that we'd discuss it in the morning. He was still up and still worried when I went to bed in the tack room, and he was gone when I woke up the next morning."

"What the hell happened while you were out for dinner?"

"I don't know," I said. "It stands to reason that he got suspicious about Tyrone. He couldn't have doped it out from the photos, because he never saw the one you sent to Billy Paulson. All I can come up with is that someone said something to him. It obviously wasn't Bigelow, and I don't think Frank Standish knows to this day that it wasn't the real Trojan colt."

"Who else would talk to him about it?" asked Chessman.

"I was hoping you might be able to tell me," I said.

A suspicious look crossed his pudgy face. "Just a minute," he growled. "Are you accusing me?"

"No, I'm not," I said. "I'm hoping you can point me in the right direction."

He lowered his head in thought for a moment, then looked up. "It's got to be a vet," he said. "The Trojan colt probably had to be euthanized, though it's always possible he got hit by lightning or ran head-first into a tree or a building in the dark. So there are some circumstances under which you didn't have to have a vet to put him down. But you'd need an experienced vet to duplicate the scar."

"I agree."

Suddenly he smiled. "And one more thing."

"What?"

"It can't be Lucius McGowan."

"Who's Lucius McGowan?" I asked.

"My vet. Mill Creek was one of his clients when I was there, but Frank wanted his own vet, the guy he'd been working with, and we had an opening for a full-timer here. I mean, hell, we're standing Pit Boss and Marauder, which comes to about fifty or sixty million dollars' worth for just those two."

"Okay," I said. "Why couldn't it be McGowan?"

He grinned again. "Because McGowan patched up the real Trojan colt while I was at Mill Creek. He knows which side the scar was on. Whoever put the scar on the ringer never saw the colt but worked from the flopped photo."

"Goddamn!" I said, returning his smile. "I should have talked to you about this sooner! Except that I hadn't doped out that it was a ringer until this morning."

He shook his head in wonderment. "A ringer at the Select Sale. No one in the world would have thought it. These are blue-blooded people selling their blue-blooded horses." He paused. "Well, all you have to do is find the vet."

"How many are there in the Lexington area?"

"Oh, Lord, I don't know," he said. "Five hundred? A thousand? With the billions of dollars of horseflesh in this area, this is the one spot in the country where it can be a big-money job for a lot of them."

"Makes finding a needle in a haystack seem easy," I said, and then a thought struck me. "There's something I haven't mentioned."

"What is it?"

"The night Tony disappeared he drove his car over to the Leestown Road Kroger."

"The supermarket?"

I nodded. "Yeah. And here's the interesting thing. It had rained on his way there and was clearly going to rain on and off all night—but he left the top down on his convertible, as if whatever he was doing only figured to take a couple of minutes."

"Now, that's interesting."

"I'll tell you something else interesting," I said. "A couple of days later I was shot at by a guy who was parked about two blocks from there."

"Same case?" he asked.

I nodded. "Same case."

"Let me guess," said Chessman. "Was he parked in front of a red brick condo complex?" He gave me the name of the nearest cross street.

"How did you know?"

"Didn't you check who lives there?"

"A couple of doctors, a lawyer, and a banker, or something like that."

Chessman smiled again. "Yeah? Well, one of those doctors is . . . well, was . . . a horse doctor."

"Oh?"

"Not anymore," said Chessman. "His name's Tobias Branson. He got ruled off the track and lost his license for supplying some very illegal performance-enhancing drugs to some very unethical trainers. He can't practice in any of the fifty states. Which, I might add, doesn't prevent him from making a good living off the industry."

"Explain," I said, starting to get very excited.

"Well, for example, the Jockey Club won't recognize artificial insemination. You can't register a foal that's conceived that way. But if you're an unethical breeder, and some mare has shipped in and either she doesn't like your stallion or he doesn't like her, and you don't want to kiss the stud fee good-bye, you might wait until three in the morning, put the mare in the stallion's proximity, collect the sperm, administer it to the mare, and voilà."

He paused and took a sip of his beer. "You want another?" He continued. "You know how Olympic distance runners oxygenate their blood? It's illegal, but it doesn't show up on tests, because it's nothing but blood and oxygen. Take a colt that keeps fading seventy yards from the wire, oxygenate his blood, and if things go right you not only win a purse but collect some heavy winnings at the window."

"Fascinating," I said as dinner arrived.

His face hardened. "Now you have to understand, Eli: this guy is a pariah. No one knows him, no one talks to him, no one acknowledges his existence . . . until they need him, and there are always a few unethical scumbags in every sport and every business who have no regard for the rules and make everyone else look bad. What I'm saying is that I know who he is, but that neither I, nor Frank Standish, nor anyone we associate with has anything to do with Branson or anyone like him. The reason I know his address is because one of the first things everyone in the business learns is to steer clear of it."

I signaled to Tilly for another beer.

"I need a minute to consider this and dope it all out," I said to Chessman.

"Just dope it out right. There are two nice kids who aren't celebrating any more birthdays. I want that bastard I used to work for brought down, and brought down hard."

I juggled it all around in my mind for a few minutes while Tilly brought me my beer and I downed about half of it.

"You know what I think?" I said.

"What?"

"According to Combes, the guard, the horse had a visitor, a potential buyer, while I was gone for dinner," I said. "A fat guy with white hair."

"Could be Branson," said Chessman. "The description fits."

"I think the one who had the visitor was Tony. I think it was Branson. He operates on the wrong side of the tracks. He knew what the colt would be worth, and he's probably been bleeding Bigelow ever since he put the scar on the ringer. Maybe he thought the horse would bring two million; that's the figure I heard when I was hired to provide security. But let's say the new owner or the underbidder mentions that they'll go to three million for him, and Branson finds out. He goes to Bigelow and asks for an extra hundred grand or so. And Bigelow stalls . . . and suddenly, the day before the auction, Branson figures out that Bigelow has got him targeted. So he tells Tony the truth, and says to make it public if anything happens to him."

"I don't buy that at all," said Chessman.

"It makes sense," I insisted.

"Maybe for a normal man," replied Chessman. "But not for Branson. You know how he got ruled off? The track vets never spotted what he'd done. He got caught because he couldn't keep his mouth shut about what a genius he is. He told one too many people about how his oxygenated blood and various drugs escaped detection." He smiled at me. "You want a more likely scenario? He stopped by to see his handiwork on the colt's neck and had to brag about it, had to say something about how his handi-work made him the Leonardo of the veterinary trade."

"And loyal, honest Tony challenges it, and Branson drops his name and credentials," I said excitedly. "Tony's so protective of the sport and of his employer that he won't discuss it with me until he can verify what he's heard. So after I go to sleep, he looks up Branson's address in a phone book or gets it from someone else—after all, from what you say, Branson's not making any effort to keep it secret. So Tony drives over to his place to make sure he was telling the truth—and then, if he was, Tony would report it. Yeah, I can buy that."

"Are you saying Branson killed both kids? Hell, he didn't even know Billy."

I thought about it for a few seconds. "Okay, it makes even more sense this way. Bigelow's run through all the normal channels to raise money, so he borrows it from the mob, and the Trojan colt is his col-lateral. Then the colt dies, he sees he's got another chestnut that's a look-alike, he tells them his plan. Maybe it's even the mob that suggests Branson."

"Go on," said Chessman, leaning forward.

"When Billy Paulsen tries to extort more money, Bigelow doesn't have to lift a finger himself. He just tells the mob, and they send a hitter named Horatio Jimenez here to kill him and protect their investment."

"Why do you think it was that particular killer?"

"Because he's the one who shot at me near Branson's condo," I answered. Anyway, maybe Branson just shoots off his mouth to Tony. Or maybe he spots Jimenez and figures the mob is going to take care of any loose ends, which means Jimenez is here to kill him before he can open his big mouth. It makes no difference."

"Why not?"

"Because both ways work, which is to say, they both lead to the same thing. Let's say Branson spots Jimenez at the sale. He has no place to run—like you say, he's a pariah—and he tells Tony that the colt's a ringer and to tell the cops and the Jockey Club if anything happens to him. But it works out the same way if he has no idea who Jimenez is, he doesn't know there's a hit on him, and he just says a little more than he should to Tony. Either way he goes home, Tony's a moral kid who loves the sport and wants to make his living in it. He decides to make sure that Branson wasn't just drunk or bullshitting before he goes to the authorities, so he goes to Branson's condo to confront him. Jimenez is hiding there. Either he overhears Tony and realizes that he has to kill them both, or else Tony walks in on the killing and Branson can't let an eyewitness walk."

"My God!" whispered Chessman. "That sounds so damned believable!"

"Was Branson married?" I asked.

"Not for years. She couldn't stand the bastard either."

"Okay," I said. "But Jimenez doesn't know it. He moves the bodies out of there—it's dark and it's raining, and if he wraps each of them in a big plastic garbage bag, who'd know what the hell they were? And since he doesn't know if there's a Mrs. Branson, or a young son home from college or the army, his employers tell him to station himself there for a few days, just in case—and when I spot his car and slow down almost to a stop to write down his plate number he starts shooting."

"Why did you want his plate number?"

"He was driving a distinctive car, and he'd taken a shot at me earlier at my motel, either because I'd spoken to you or more likely because I'd already driven around the area near the Kroger's lot trying to figure out what the hell Tony had been doing there."

"So he's still on the loose and we could both be in danger right now?" asked Chessman, suddenly peering into the parking lot.

"No, you're not in any danger," I assured him.

"How do you know?"

"You were gone when Branson did his work on the colt, and just knowing that Branson exists isn't a killing offense. Besides, if I could walk in on you twice in the past couple of days, don't you think Jimenez could if he wanted to?"

"You've got a point," he admitted, relaxing visibly.

"Anyway, I'm going directly to the police station from here, and then some uniformed friends and I will decide on our next move. But in the end, Bigelow—and Jimenez, if he hasn't flown the coop yet—are going down."

"I've watched enough mystery shows on television to ask: don't you have to have a body to charge someone with murder?"

I nodded my head. "Yeah, you do. We'll have three—the two grooms and Branson."

He looked completely puzzled. "Where?"

"I wasn't sure when the day started," I told him. Then I smiled. "But I know now."

32.

After I dropped Chessman off at Blue Banner Farm I went back to the station. Berger and Bernice were still there, though I didn't know if they were on duty or just waiting to hear what I'd learned.

I laid it out for them, and they agreed with my conclusions.

"I'm going to arrest that son of a bitch tonight," announced Berger.

"Which one?" asked Bernice with a smile.

"Bigelow," he said. "We'll stake out Branson's condo too, just in case, and put out an APB on Jimenez before we leave." He picked up his phone. "Sam? Lou. We're gonna take Bigelow down tonight. Get me a court order to bust in if I have to . . . hell, I don't know. Make it a search warrant, and say we're looking for the real Trojan colt."

He hung up and turned to me. "We've got a couple of understanding local judges. Sam'll contact one of them, and he should be back with a warrant in fifteen or twenty minutes. Why don't you two grab some dinner or something, while I line up a couple of boys in blue and a paddy wagon?"

"Hell, no!" I said. "I started this investigation. I'm going to be in on the end of it."

"The end of it is probably a two-year attempt to extradite Jimenez from New Mexico once he runs back there and thirty mob members swear he never left."

"I'm coming with you!" I insisted.

"So am I," said Bernice.

He shrugged and turned to Bernice. "I know better than to argue with you," he said. "Keep your blues on."

She nodded and turned to me. "Let him make all his arrangements and we'll get ourselves some coffee."

"Sounds good," I said.

"And he'd damned well better not try leaving without us," she added, raising her voice.

He put a pained expression on his face, then picked up his phone and went to work as we walked down the hall to get some coffee.

"So Jimenez isn't working for Bigelow!" she said. "That one got right by me, but of course given his financial situation he couldn't pay for a high-priced hitter."

"And the end result is the same," I added. "Anyone he wants to get rid of, it's in the mob's best interest to do the dirty work for him."

"At least until the check for the colt clears," she said.

"He sold it to one of those Dubai oil sheikhs," I said. "The guy probably makes more in a day than what the colt cost. It must be a nice life."

"Yeah," she said dubiously. "But he can't watch Big Blue go up against Louisville."

"My mistake," I said with a smile. "I don't know what I could have been thinking."

She laughed, we talked a bit more and were about to return to Berger's office when he emerged from it and approached us.

"Everything's set," he said. "You want to ride in the squad car or the paddy wagon?"

"Why don't we just take my own car and follow you?" I said. "That way if you're stuck there for a few hours, we can leave once he's under arrest."

He shrugged. "Suit yourself."

We turned and fell into step behind him as he walked to the front entrance. The paddy wagon was parked just a few feet away, its motor idling. Lou walked over to a squad car, and Bernice and I went to the Camry. Night had fallen and we needed the headlights. We fell into formation behind them as we all drove out—I hoped for the last time—to Mill Creek Farm.

It was obvious as we pulled up to the house that something was wrong. The door was open, and Hector the doorman was lying unconscious about ten feet to the right on it. Sounds emanated from the house, sounds like someone was getting the crap beat out of him.

We rushed in through the foyer and then to the living room. Travis Bigelow was tied to a chair, blood streaming down his face. Horatio Jimenez was working him over, screaming, "Where is it, you lying bastard?"

"That's enough!" I said, starting to approach them.

Jimenez turned and rushed at me. A single shot rang out, and he fell to the floor, bellowing in pain, and I could see a huge bloody stain spreading out from his knee. I turned and saw that Bernice had her gun in her hand, aimed at him.

"You kneecapped me, you goddamned puta!" he roared, pulling his gun out of his shoulder holster.

There was another explosion, and his gun went flying through the air and he screamed again as blood began spurting from his hand.

"Call me a puta again and you may have to learn how to sign your autograph with your nose," said Bernice pleasantly. Then, to no one in particular, she added: "I no longer resent all those hours at the shooting range."

"Call an ambulance," said Berger to one of the officers. "And ride with him to the hospital to make sure he doesn't try any funny stuff. We'll arrange for a twenty-four-hour guard once he's there."

The officer nodded, pulled out his cell phone, and called 911 on it.

"All right, Mr. Bigelow," said Berger as he went over and began untying him. "You'll make a side trip to the hospital, but then you're going to jail. Let me guess: you not only promised the three million, or a substantial portion of it, to Jimenez's employers, but to a bunch of other people as well." He smiled. "You've been a very bad boy."

"Those are my private dealings," mumbled Bigelow weakly but defiantly. "His employers aren't going to press charges, and neither are you."

"You got it all wrong," said Berger. "We don't care if you rob the mob. But you ran a ringer in the sale, and you're going to jail for it."

"I won't admit to a damned thing," whispered Bigelow as we heard the siren of an approaching ambulance.

"You don't have to," answered Berger. "We'll just run a DNA test on the colt." Bigelow's swollen eyes widened—well, as much as they could—in surprise, and Berger chuckled. "Welcome to the twenty-first century, Mr. Bigelow."

Then they were loading Jimenez and Bigelow onto a pair of stretchers, and Berger had both of his officers ride along with them.

"Where's Mrs. Bigelow?" asked Bernice.

"I checked before we came out there," answered Berger. "She's in New York, spending money she doesn't have on things she doesn't need."

"Well, that's that," she said, finally putting her gun away.

"Not quite," said Berger. He turned to me. "So where are the bodies?"

"Follow me," I said.

I walked out of the house and headed toward the largest barn, the one that housed Frank Standish's office. We walked past the huge backhoe, and just before we reached the barn I stopped.

"Right there," I said, pointing to the little equine cemetery.

"Silk Scarf?" he said, shining a flashlight on the small cement marker.

"She died this spring, so the grave is fresh. It hasn't had time for anything to grow on it, so it was easy to open it up without anyone paying any attention. He did it the night the colt sold, when he paid Standish to take the night staff out to dinner and the movies."

"You'd better be right," said Berger.

"I am," I replied confidently.

"What the hell," he said. "Even if you're wrong, we've still got Bigelow on a felony, and we'll have plenty on Jimenez before he's healthy enough to move. We'll wait here for some replacements to arrive, and then I'm buying you and Annie Oakley here a drink."

The next morning, armed with a court order to go with the previous night's search warrant, they opened the grave and found three bodies—Billy Paulson, Tobias Branson, and Tony Sanders—just atop that of Silk Scarf. Then they dug a little farther down and found the remains of a young colt with a broken foreleg.

I reported the sad news to Tony's parents, had one last dinner with Bernice, and drove home.

EPILOGUE

Some people have strange senses of humor. Khalid Rahjan, the Arab who shelled out three and a quarter million for the colt, was one of them. He viewed the whole thing as a huge joke on himself. He never tried to return the colt, never asked for his money back, didn't even ask for a price adjustment. He even made "Tyrone" its official name. I suppose when you make a million dollars an hour on slow days, you can find humor in almost any situation.

It had been ten months since the night we arrested Bigelow and Jimenez, and they were both doing time. I'd driven down a couple of times to visit Bernice, but in January she told me that she was dating a local. MacDonald moved to some obscure little town in Utah, God knows why, and joined the force there, and Lou Berger got a commendation and transferred to headquarters.

I hadn't been back since the turn of the year, but I found myself driving down to Kentucky on a pleasant April day just to see an old friend in action. I had a late breakfast at Tilly's with Hal Chessman, and then we drove an hour over to Churchill Downs in Louisville, where they were running the Bashford Manor Stakes for two-year-olds.

The very first Trojan colt to reach the track would be making his debut. So would the first starter by the imported British champion Morpheus. And there was one other colt who'd be starting for the first time. His sire was Spellsinger, a nice but not outstanding racehorse who had sired a couple of stakes winners and a lot of losers, and his dam was a Mill Creek Farm mare named Sassy Suzie. The colt's name was Tyrone, and he was the old friend I'd come to see.

"He's 65-to-1," noted Chessman. "Figures for a nonstarter going against two of the best-bred colts in the crop. Of course," he added, "all that could change overnight."

"What do you mean?" I asked.

"Breeding's not a science," said Chessman. "Citation had a couple of full brothers who never won a race. And on the flip side, Polynesian and Bold Reasoning, who sired Native Dancer and Seattle Slew, weren't classic sires until the Dancer and Slew came along, and then overnight they were. So for all anyone knows, the best-bred colt in the field might be Tyrone."

I looked at the tote board. He was up to 80-to-1. "I don't think a lot of people agree with you."

"They're probably right," he agreed. "I'm just pointing out that nothing's written in stone. Or to coin a phrase: That's what makes horse races."

"There he is," I said, pointing to Tyrone as he walked by us in the post parade.

"He looks fit," said Chessman. "I'm going to go put ten dollars down on him. Want me to lay a bet for you?"

I looked at the board: 90-to-1. The bay by Trojan was even money, and the black Morpheus colt was 8-to-5. Which figured. They were that well-bred.

"No," I said at last. "I don't want to jinx him, I'll just root for him."

"Up to you," he replied with a shrug. He was back in three or four minutes, clutching his ticket in his hand.

Then they were in the gate, and a few seconds later the bell rang, the doors opened, and the Morpheus colt shot out to a lead, tracked by the favorite. I didn't have any binoculars, and Khalid Rahjan's silks were a dull color, hard to spot. I had no idea where Tyrone was until they turned into the homestretch. Then a sleek chestnut circled the field, caught the leaders with an eighth of a mile to go, and began pulling away from him. I still didn't recognize his silks, but I couldn't miss the scar on his neck.

Chessman cashed his ticket, teased me all the way back to Lexington, and then I drove home.

They say dogs can't laugh. Bullshit. Marlowe spent the whole night laughing at me.

ABOUT THE AUTHOR

MIKE RESNICK is the all-time leading award-winner for short fiction in science fiction history and is the author of seventy-one novels, over two hundred fifty short stories, and three screenplays, as well as the editor of forty-one anthologies. A number of those novels and stories were mysteries set in the future or on other worlds. But Mike doesn't limit himself to science fiction, as fans of *Dog in the Manger* know, and Seventh Street Books is pleased to have enticed him back to contemporary mysteries with *The Trojan Colt*. Visit him online at www.mikeresnick.com, at www.facebook.com/mike.resnick1, and on Twitter @ResnickMike.